A Note from Stephanie About the Hot New Gossip Column

Some secrets are hard to keep to yourself—especially this one! I'm the writer of the school paper's gossip column, and nobody is supposed to find out—not even my best friends, Darcy and Allie. But secrets can sometimes get you into trouble. . . .

Before I tell you about the big mess I got myself into, let me tell you about my big family. My *very* big family.

Right now there are nine people and a dog living in our house—and for all I know, someone new could move in at any time. There's me, my big sister, D.J., my little sister, Michelle, and my dad, Danny. But that's just the beginning.

Uncle Jesse came first. My dad asked him to come live with us when my mom died, to help take care of me and my sisters.

Back then, Uncle Jesse didn't know much about taking care of three little girls. He was more into rock 'n' roll. So Dad asked his old college buddy, Joey Gladstone, to help out. Joey didn't know anything about kids, either—but it sure was funny watching him learn!

Having Uncle Jesse and Joey around was like having three dads instead of one! But then something even better happened—Uncle Jesse fell in love. He married Becky Donaldson, Dad's co-host on his TV show, *Wake Up, San Francisco*. Aunt Becky's so nice—she's more like a big sister than an aunt.

Next Uncle Jesse and Aunt Becky had twin baby boys. Their names are Nicky and Alex, and they are adorable!

I love being part of a big family. Still, things can get pretty crazy when you live in such a full house!

FULL HOUSE™: STEPHANIE novels

Phone Call from a Flamingo
The Boy-Oh-Boy Next Door
Twin Troubles
Hip Hop Till You Drop
Here Comes the Brand-New Me
The Secret's Out

Available from MINSTREL Books

FULL HOUSE™
Stephanie

The Secret's Out

Katie Kimball

A Parachute Press Book

A MINSTREL® BOOK

PUBLISHED BY POCKET BOOKS

New York   London   Toronto   Sydney   Tokyo   Singapore

This book is a work of fiction. Names, characters, places, and incidents are products of the author's imagination or are used fictitiously. Any resemblance to actual events or locales or persons, living or dead, is entirely coincidental.

A MINSTREL PAPERBACK *Original*

 POCKET BOOKS, a division of Simon & Schuster Inc.
1230 Avenue of the Americas, New York, NY 10020

A Parachute Press Book
Copyright © 1994 by Lorimar Television, Inc.

FULL HOUSE, characters, names and all related indicia are trademarks of Lorimar Television © 1994.

All rights reserved, including the right to reproduce this book or portions thereof in any form whatsoever. For information address Pocket Books, 1230 Avenue of the Americas, New York, NY 10020

ISBN: 0-671-89859-0

First Minstrel Books printing November 1994

10 9 8 7 6 5 4 3 2 1

A MINSTREL BOOK and colophon are registered trademarks of Simon & Schuster Inc.

Cover photo by Schultz Photography

Printed in the U.S.A.

The Secret's Out

CHAPTER

1

◆ ◀ ◆ ◆

"I don't believe this," Stephanie Tanner said. She was sitting with her best friends, Allie Taylor and Darcy Powell, at their usual table in the cafeteria.

"What don't you believe?" Allie asked. "You mean this story in the paper?" Allie's head was buried in the *Scribe*, the school's weekly newspaper, which came out on Fridays. She didn't notice that Stephanie was staring into her lunch bag.

"Not the paper. *This*," Stephanie said, pulling a glump of brown mush wrapped in plastic out of her sack. "I squashed my peanut butter sandwich again."

"Disgusting," Allie agreed, without looking up from the newspaper. "Wow! Look at this!"

"What?" Darcy asked. She was slender and graceful, and her purple sweater set off her dark skin. Her golden brown eyes lit up with curiosity as she leaned across the table to peer at Allie's copy of the paper.

"Right here in The Secret's Out, the gossip column!" Allie said, tucking a strand of wavy, light brown hair behind her ear. "It says, 'A seventh-grade soccer player's pants split open on the field during practice last week.' And get this!" she squealed. " 'He was wearing *Bugs Bunny* underwear!"

"No way!" Darcy giggled. "That's so dorky!"

"It *is* pretty funny, though, don't you think?" Stephanie asked, watching their expressions with a sly smile.

"Sure, it's funny, as long as it's not *your* underwear!" Allie said, laughing.

Darcy bit into her apple and looked at Stephanie. "You work on the school paper, Steph. You must know who the mystery writer is for the gossip column."

Stephanie got busy pulling the plastic wrap away from her mashed sandwich and avoided looking into her friend's eyes.

"Well?" Darcy said. "Who is it?"

"Umm . . ." Stephanie said. She'd won her spot on the *Scribe* staff by entering a funny story in the paper's writing contest just a few weeks ago. "I haven't been working there very long, you know."

Allie leaned toward Stephanie and whispered, "It's probably supposed to be a secret, but you can tell us anyway. We're your best friends in the whole world."

Stephanie hesitated, twisting a strand of long blond hair around her finger. She felt like screaming, *It's me! I write The Secret's Out!* But even though she was *dying* to tell her friends, she just couldn't. Brenda Mason, the newspaper editor, had told Stephanie she absolutely couldn't tell anyone that she was writing it. "Sorry," Stephanie said. "I'm sworn to secrecy. Everybody who works on the newspaper is. I mean, the writer has to be anonymous so she can get the gossip without anybody knowing."

"*She?*" Darcy said.

"Or he," Stephanie added quickly.

Allie and Darcy exchanged suspicious glances.

"Well, what do *you* do for the paper?" Darcy asked.

Only two seventh graders had been asked to join the staff—Stephanie and Sue Kramer. Sue did general reporting, but because Stephanie had a great sense of humor and no one else wanted the job, she got to write the gossip column. It was the most exciting thing that had ever happened to her! Only problem was, she couldn't tell anyone. "Oh, you know," she said with a shrug. "I do different things."

"Like what?" Allie asked, popping a potato chip into her mouth.

"Like . . . like occasional reporting and feature pieces."

Darcy's dark eyebrows rose in surprise. "Really? I didn't see your name on any of the articles."

"That's because I didn't do any for this issue." Stephanie licked a fingerful of peanut butter, then worked loose a big glump of sandwich. "I'll have some important pieces coming up soon."

"I can't wait to see them," Allie said. "But even if you just type stuff or run errands, it's still pretty cool to be working on the paper."

It's cooler than you know, Stephanie wanted to say. But she kept her lips clamped together and nodded in silent agreement.

"Oh, no!" Darcy squealed. She'd picked up the paper and started reading more of The Secret's Out. "Look at this one! 'R.B. has a crush on Mr. Assante, the new English teacher and seventh-grade class adviser.' "

"Whoever R.B. is, I don't blame her," Allie said. "Mr. Assante's really good looking." She pointed across the cafeteria. Tall and dark haired, Mr. Assante was talking and laughing with a group of kids. "He's nice, too."

"Yeah, he is," Stephanie agreed. "And he actually treats us like real people. I guess that's why everybody likes him so much."

"Listen!" Darcy said, still reading the gossip column. "Here's one about someone with the initials D.L. It says, 'D.L. skipped school to go surfing!' "

"Wow! Is D.L. going to be in trouble when Principal Thomas reads that!" Allie said, shaking her head.

"I'm sure there are plenty of D.L.'s in the school," Stephanie murmured hopefully. *And I sure hope he doesn't mind that I wrote that about him,* she added silently.

"But how many kids have been absent in the last two weeks?" Allie pointed out. "It's got to be Daniel Lappes. Mr. Thomas will have no trouble tracking him down."

"Wait! Look at the next part," Darcy said, bouncing up and down in her chair. She forgot all about her lunch in her excitement. "It's about the seventh grade's annual class party!"

"What about it?" Allie asked.

Stephanie smiled smugly. This was the best thing she'd written for the column. She was so glad she'd overheard those two kids in the hallway talking about the party.

" 'Rumor has it,' " Darcy read, " 'the location of this year's seventh-grade class party will be Fun City Amusement Park!' Do you believe that!"

"Fun City!" Allie gasped. "They have the neatest roller coaster called the Tyrannosaur! I mean it's just humongous. And there's tons of food, and a water slide, and a double Ferris wheel, and—"

"Hey, guys," Stephanie said. "Calm down. It's only a rumor."

"What's with you?" Darcy asked, frowning at Stephanie. "I think it's cool that we're going to have our party there."

"Me too!" Allie agreed, her green eyes sparkling.

Stephanie smiled at her friends. Who knew, it might turn out to be true! She finished her milk, then stuffed the straw down into the carton and looked up to find Allie and Darcy still deep in discussion about the party at the amusement park.

"There's even a section in the video arcade of virtual reality machines—like, you make the games do anything you want!" Allie said, so loudly that kids from the next table turned to see what she was talking about.

Two seventh-grade boys got up and walked over. "Did you say something about a party at Fun City?" Jason Tobin asked.

"That would be the coolest party ever," Brent Meacham said, sitting down beside Stephanie. To her horror, she realized he was the boy whose pants had split on the soccer field. She wondered briefly if he was wearing Bugs Bunny underpants today, but decided she couldn't ask.

What would he do to her if he found out she'd been the one to write about him in the newspaper? Wasn't it bad enough that he'd been embarrassed in front of more than fifty kids at the game? Now the whole school knew . . . because of her. But she'd needed some newsbreaking stuff, and Brent's underwear had been pretty funny.

"Hey, Steph, why are you being so quiet?" Darcy asked. "Aren't you psyched about Fun City?"

"Yeah," Jason agreed. "This will be a first for the seventh grade. We've always had the party by the fishpond at the park."

"Bo-ring," Brent moaned.

"Super-bo-ring," Jason agreed.

"I can't wait!" Allie cried excitedly. "The party's only two months away."

"I hear the Tyrannosaur is totally wild," Brent said.

"It must be great," Jason added. "My little brother barfed when he went on it."

Stephanie laughed along with the others, secretly thrilled that kids were reading her column. All she had to do was write a few lines of gossip and the whole school was talking about it. This was one secret that was going to be hard to keep!

The night it was Stephanie's turn to set the table at the Tanner house. While she laid out forks, knives, and spoons, she tried to come up with some new stories for the gossip column. The deadline was Monday.

"What's for supper?" eight-year-old Michelle asked, crossing the room and flopping into one of the chairs at the long kitchen table. Comet, the family's golden retriever, followed her in and sat by her feet. "Comet and I are hungry."

"I think Becky made a macaroni-and-cheese casserole," Stephanie said. Becky Donaldson co-hosted the TV show *Wake Up, San Francisco* with Stephanie's father, Danny. Becky was married to Danny's brother-in-law, Jesse. Becky and Jesse had twin three-year-old boys, Nicky and Alex, and lived on the top floor of the house.

Stephanie continued setting the table for the family—all nine of them. It seemed as if the family just grew and grew, but Stephanie liked it that way. There was always someone around to talk to. Maybe her family could help her come up with some interesting stories for the paper.

When dinner was ready, everyone sat down and started talking about the day.

"My pre-calculus test this afternoon was the hardest ever," D.J. complained. She was a senior in high school, taking college-prep courses. "I just know I messed up on it big-time."

"That means you got a *B*," Stephanie teased. "You never get really bad grades."

"I don't know . . ." D.J. spread butter on a slice of bread and took a bite. "It was pretty awful."

"Back when I was your age, I had a math teacher named Mrs. Murphy," said Stephanie's father, Danny, launching into one of his many stories about the good old days. "Talk about hard tests! Hers were the worst. I remember studying a whole week for one and I still only got a *B* minus."

Joey made a funny face. "Are you going to start that again? We could sit here all night while you remember every one of your old teachers."

Stephanie was used to her dad's stories, but she had to admit she sometimes found Joey's stories funnier. He was a comedian, and he told the corniest jokes around the dinner table.

"Hey, Joey," she said, "why did the chicken cross the playground?"

"Duh, I don't know, Steph. Why did he?" Joey asked.

"To get to the other slide!"

Joey rolled his eyes. "How about this one. Why do firemen wear red suspenders?"

"I don't know," Stephanie said.

"To hold up their pants!" Joey shouted.

Everyone groaned.

"Don't you have any new jokes?" Michelle asked.

"It's an oldie but a goodie," Danny said, laughing. He turned to Stephanie. "Tell us about your day, honey."

"Well, you know how I'm writing for the school newspaper," Stephanie began. "The thing is, the editor, this really bossy eighth grader named Brenda Mason, gave me the job of writing

10

the gossip column because no one else ⟩
do it."

"Why not?" D.J. asked.

"She said the last three writers quit because they couldn't come up with enough good ideas for the column. One of them even wrote about the school janitor's collection of bottle caps."

Jesse grinned. "That is pretty dull."

Stephanie nodded. "Well, I figured I'd find tons of interesting and fun things to write about people at school. I mean, there's always lots of stuff going on; it's just finding out what's happening soon enough so that it's still hot news."

"So what's the problem?" D.J. asked.

"The problem is, I have to come up with more stories, like real fast. The next edition goes to press soon, and I don't know what to write. I'll lose my job if I don't come up with something."

"Hey, no sweat," Jesse said. "If all of us put our heads together, we ought to be able to think of some great stuff."

"What about news of someone running for class office?" Danny suggested.

"Isn't that sort of dry for a fun column?" Jesse asked. "How about something on the cheerleaders? Any klutzes on the squad?"

"Well," Stephanie said thoughtfully, "I guess I could say something about one of them, without naming names, of course."

"Like she slipped on a banana peel in the cafeteria?" Michelle suggested. "But did a perfect flip and landed on her feet?"

Stephanie laughed. Taking a small notebook out of her jeans pocket, she clicked open her pen. "Maybe I could use that, Michelle. What else?"

"How about Tammy Ash and Freddie Maples?" asked D.J.

"What about them?"

"I heard they were going to be related soon!"

"Married, in seventh grade?" Stephanie gasped. "That's ridiculous!"

"Not married," D.J. said. "Tammy's mom and Freddie's dad are both divorced, but they've been dating each other. They may be getting married— at least that's what I heard Tammy's older sister say."

"Wow!" Stephanie wrote faster. "That's a definite scoop. Kids love finding out family secrets."

"But you have to make sure it's true," Danny cautioned her. "You wouldn't want to lie."

"Oh, Dad, don't worry," she said. "I'll use initials, like before. It's the story that counts."

"You could write something about someone's little brother or sister," Michelle said.

"Like what?"

"Like how I'm going to be a pumpkin in the third-grade play." Michelle picked up her plastic glass and took a long drink of milk. As she started to put down her glass, Stephanie's hand shot out to stop her. "What's that?" Stephanie asked.

"What's what?" Michelle said.

"On the bottom of your glass—something's written there."

Michelle held the plastic tumbler over her head so they could all see what was written on the bottom: Fun City.

"Where did you get that?" Stephanie asked.

"Dad," Michelle said proudly.

"We did a special piece on the park this morning for the show," Danny said. "It's a great place for families."

"It is," Becky agreed. "I actually went on a few of the rides, and they were a lot of fun."

"And the place is kept absolutely spotless," Danny added. He was the neat freak in the family. "They scrub out their popcorn poppers every night after closing. And they have a full-time staff of caretakers who sweep the walkways, remove trash, and sanitize the rest rooms every hour, as long as the park is open. Why, I wouldn't mind taking you guys there someday!"

"When! When! When!" Michelle shouted.

"When! When! When!" Nicky and Alex echoed her.

"I think you've made a big mistake," Becky said, laughing. "You've started something."

"Let me think about it," Danny said. "We'll try to go sometime soon."

Fun City sounded cool, Stephanie thought as she started clearing the table. It would be great if the seventh grade really could go there for the class party. But her problem right now was coming up with a story big enough to top her Fun City and Bugs Bunny stories. It had to be something special, something really juicy. And she had to think fast—her column was due Monday.

CHAPTER
2

♦ ◀ ◗ ♦

Stephanie banged her locker shut and raced down the hallway to the office where the newspaper staff was holding its Monday meeting. The deadline for her column was today. The ideas her family had suggested had been funny, but she'd decided they weren't the sort of thing she could use. They just weren't *juicy* enough.

Brenda is really going to be steamed, Stephanie thought.

"Whoa, Stephanie, where's the fire?" Mr. Assante asked as she flew around a corner and almost bumped into him.

"Oh, hi, Mr. Assante," Stephanie said breathlessly. "Sorry. I've got to get to the newspaper office. I'm late with a story."

"Well, try to get there in one piece," he said with a smile, stepping out of her way.

Stephanie grinned and hurried on. Behind her, she heard two kids asking Mr. Assante about the class party at Fun City. *Great,* she thought. Everybody was reading her column.

When she got to the newspaper office, almost everyone was already there. Most of the kids were eighth and ninth graders. Stephanie felt really lucky to be one of the two seventh graders on the staff.

Brenda looked up from the pages in her hand when Stephanie walked in. "You're finally here, Tanner. Good," Brenda said. "Got your column all ready?"

"Not exactly," Stephanie said hesitantly.

Brenda looked surprised. "What do you mean, *not exactly?*"

"Well, it's still in the planning stages."

Brenda rolled her eyes and looked at the boy standing closest to her.

"I have to enter all the articles on the computer this afternoon," he said.

Stephanie's mouth went dry. What was she going to do? She couldn't just make stuff up!

Brenda turned back to her. "Think you can handle this job, Stephanie?"

"I—I can handle it," Stephanie stammered. "I just need a few minutes to get my notes together. The rest is all up here." She pointed to her head, which was suddenly pounding.

"All right," Brenda said. "Sit down and get to work. As soon as you have your column together, hand it to Gary."

Stephanie swallowed. "You mean I have to write it *right now*? Here?"

"Here and now or not at all," Brenda said. "You're past deadline already!"

Stephanie collapsed into the nearest chair and dropped her book bag on the floor. A knot tightened up in her stomach as she pulled a pencil out of her book bag and ripped a sheet of paper from her spiral notebook.

She stared at the blank paper.

Nothing came to mind.

She took a big breath, letting it out slowly. *What am I going to write?* she asked herself frantically.

From somewhere down the hallway, the sound of the concert choir drifted to her. They were rehearsing for Parents' Night. Their voices broke into her favorite song, a bouncy version of a new Mariah Carey tune. Stephanie started tapping her foot to the beat, finding it harder and harder to sit still.

The music stopped. Stephanie looked at her pencil. The tip didn't look very sharp. She got up and crossed the room to the sharpener and gave her pencil a perfect point. On her way back to the desk, she saw the water fountain outside in the hallway. Suddenly she felt very thirsty, and she slipped outside for a quick drink.

When she stepped back into the room, Brenda looked up from her work. "What are you *doing?*" she demanded.

Startled, Stephanie jumped, and a cold sweat seeped into her T-shirt. "I was just, umm . . . getting ready to write," she said meekly.

"Well, quit getting *ready* to write and *write!*" Brenda grumbled. She swung away to answer one of her reporters' questions.

With a heavy heart, Stephanie focused on the blank sheet of paper. This was really hard. But Brenda wouldn't let her leave until she'd written her column. And she couldn't very well stay all night.

Resolved to do her best, she set the tip of her pencil on the paper. Maybe she should write a story about Brenda being so bossy.... No, that would just make her angry.

Stephanie thought about her day. What had happened that had been interesting? She'd gone swimming in gym. And Mary Kelly had gotten a pass to go to the nurse's office so she wouldn't have to take gym. Mary was one of the seventh-grade members of the Flamingoes, a group of girls who thought they were the coolest kids in school. Hadn't Mary gotten a nurse's pass last time too? And the time before that? And each day she'd been back in their next class, looking just fine.

Stephanie wrote: *A certain seventh-grade Flamingo gets excuses from the nurse three times a week to get out of swimming. Can it be that all Flamingoes don't like water? This reporter thinks this is one bird who's afraid of the wet stuff!*

She took another breath and squinted into the sunlight streaming through the classroom window. Someone in math class had told her about Coach Elwin blowing his top at a kid for cutting practice. Who was it? *Oh, that's it!* she thought.

G.H. is going to get kicked off the football team. That is, if he misses any more practices. Coach Elwin was

19

heard threatening to boot the defensive lineman when he cut his second practice in a week.

Not bad at all, Stephanie thought, feeling rather pleased with herself.

She chewed the eraser end of the pencil. This was getting easier. Stephanie thought back to a social studies class last week. Something had interrupted the test . . . what was it?

"Yes!" she whispered, and started writing feverishly. *D.M. got caught cheating on a social studies test and now has detention for two weeks.*

The ideas were flowing now. Without even taking a breath between items, she kept on writing.

Popular, hunky ninth-grader T.R. was roaming the halls between classes without a pass. When the hall monitor took off after him, he ducked into the girls' locker room. You should have heard the screams from the third-period gym class!

With a sigh of relief, Stephanie scooped up her pages and dropped her pencil into her book bag. *That wasn't so hard*, she thought. *All I had to do was stick to the facts!* There were plenty of exciting things happening around school.

Stephanie stood up with the sheets of paper in hand.

"Are you done?" Brenda asked.

"Yup," said Stephanie, handing her the pages. "And it's really juicy stuff."

"Good, we need some fresh gossip to get kids to buy the paper. Our sales have been way down this year." Brenda looked at her. "Now don't wait until the last minute for next week's issue. Get started as soon as you can so you don't miss the next deadline."

"Right," Stephanie called over her shoulder as she dashed out of the room without looking back. She'd had enough of Brenda for one day.

As she turned into the hallway, she overheard two eighth graders talking about Fun City.

"I don't see why we can't have *our* class party there," the boy complained. "The seventh grade is going for the whole day!"

"I'll talk with Mrs. Morano, our class adviser," the girl said with a serious nod. "There must be some way we can go to Fun City too!"

Totally amazing! Stephanie thought. Even eighth graders were reading the column. Humming to herself, she took off for her locker. She'd have to catch the late bus now or walk. But maybe walking wouldn't be so bad after sitting there writing for so long.

She worked the combination lock on the front of

the skinny metal locker, then yanked open the door and reached for her coat. With a gasp she pulled back her hand.

Someone had slipped a note inside her locker! Cool!

Wondering who the note might be from, she read the message: *The Secret's Out, Stephanie! I know it's you, and I'm going to get you back.*

CHAPTER
3

◆ ◀ ◆ ◆

The next morning Stephanie dressed slowly for school, even though she'd decided to walk and needed extra time to get there before the bell rang. She'd lain awake for hours, wondering who had written the mysterious note and what he or she planned to do to get back at her.

She wasn't ready in time to walk with D.J. and her sister's best friend, Kimmy. They went on ahead since she was still blow drying her hair when they left.

It wasn't until she was crossing the school yard and heard the last bell ring, calling everyone to homeroom, that Stephanie realized how late she was. She raced down the hallway, grabbed her first- and second-period books out of her locker, then ran for homeroom just as all the classroom doors were swinging shut. There was no time to meet Allie and Darcy by the pay telephone outside the gym, as she usually did. Maybe she could catch up with them between homeroom and first period.

As she took her seat, Stephanie glanced around. Everyone was looking at her and laughing. One girl pointed at her and whispered something to a boy.

"What's wrong?" Stephanie asked Carrie Townsend, who sat next to her.

Carrie only giggled.

Stephanie looked down at the front of her blouse to see if she'd forgotten to do up a button or spilled cereal on it.

Everything seemed okay to her.

She glanced at Mrs. Benson, her homeroom teacher. The teacher didn't look very happy with all the noise the students were making.

"That's it, class!" she shouted at last. "Settle down so I can call roll!"

But the commotion only got louder, and one of the girls yelled, "She doesn't even see it. Let's tell her!"

"See what?" Stephanie demanded, losing her patience.

Then she saw it. Behind Mrs. Benson, drawn across the blackboard in colored chalk, was a huge picture of Bugs Bunny. Over the cartoon character's head was a balloon that read, *What's up, Stephanie? The Secret's Out, and now the whole school knows you write the gossip column.*

Stephanie felt her face flush a hot pink. She swallowed and looked around the room. Everyone was pointing at her and laughing, and now she knew why.

"Brent Meacham!" she muttered under her breath. He was the one with the Bugs Bunny underwear. He must have written the note!

She felt like running from the room. Everyone would hate her now that they knew she'd been spreading rumors and telling tales!

Maybe Brenda would kick her off the school newspaper because her cover was blown. Maybe no one would talk to her the rest of the school year.

I'll transfer to another school! she thought desperately. *It's the only solution.* She squeezed her eyes shut, wishing she could just disappear.

"Hey, Steph," a voice said from nearby, "is it really true R.B. has a crush on Mr. Assante?" It was Melissa White, on her way to her seat. "I used to have a crush on him too. But that was a couple of weeks ago."

Mrs. Benson finally saw what was on the board, and she said, "Melissa, while you're up, erase the blackboard. Then please sit down."

"I'll talk to you about it later," Stephanie whispered to Melissa.

No sooner had she turned around than the girl sitting to her right leaned across the aisle and whispered, "Guess what I heard about Mara Block?"

Stephanie stared at her. "I don't know, what?"

"Tell you later," the girl said with an air of mystery. "I'll bet you can use it in your column."

The bell for first period rang, and suddenly kids swarmed around her.

"When are we going to Fun City, Steph?"

"Yeah, have they set the date for the party yet?"

"Hey, Steph, I'll call you tonight! I have a really incredible story to tell you!"

"Me too!"

Stephanie sat at her desk in shock. What was going on? The kids weren't mad at her at all. They still liked her! They more than liked her—they were treating her like she was the most popular girl in the room!

"Time to get to your classes," Mrs. Benson reminded them. "Move along now, or you'll all be late."

Stephanie struggled up from her seat and managed to get out through the door into the hallway, even though a dozen kids were still crowded around her, shouting out ideas for the gossip column or asking if she knew anything about rumors they'd heard around the school.

Totally cool! Stephanie thought.

All Tuesday morning it seemed as if Stephanie had been at the head of a parade of students trying to find out what was new around school. "You'll just have to wait till Friday," she'd told them, "when the paper goes on sale."

And it wasn't until lunchtime that Stephanie realized she hadn't seen Darcy and Allie all morning. She spotted them across the cafeteria and made her way toward their usual table.

"Hey, where have you been all day?" Darcy asked.

"Yeah, we waited for you by the phone," Allie said.

Stephanie winced, feeling guilty for having forgotten about them after homeroom. "Sorry, I sort of got tied up."

"We heard something weird about you," Darcy said, looking at her with a puzzled expression.

"Well, not really weird, just surprising," Allie added in a quiet voice. "I mean, since we're your best friends in the whole world, we know more about you than anyone else, and—"

Darcy broke in. "Jenni Morris said you're the writer for the gossip column in the *Scribe*."

"It's not true, is it?" Allie asked.

"Well . . ." Stephanie began.

From across the cafeteria a group of girls ran over to their table. Stephanie couldn't believe it when she realized that three of the Flamingoes were standing across the table from her. She glanced at Darcy and Allie and saw that they were pretty amazed too.

"I can't wait for the next gossip column to come out," Jenni Morris said in a snide voice. Jenni was the leader of the Flamingoes, and she and Stephanie had never gotten along.

The other two girls nodded in agreement.

"It must be so cool, getting all the dirt on people," Jenni said. "How did *you* ever get a job like that?"

Stephanie opened her mouth to answer her, but one of Jenni's friends pressed a note into Stephanie's hand. "You'll never believe what it says," she whispered. "Every word of it is true. I heard it from one of my closest friends, who got it from her cousin, who's an eighth grader."

The three girls walked away.

"I guess we heard right," Allie murmured to Stephanie. "You *are* the gossip column writer."

"Yeah, I am," Stephanie admitted.

Allie and Darcy exchanged disappointed looks.

"Listen, I would have told you guys," Stephanie said, "but Brenda said it was supposed to be a secret."

"Well, it's not a secret anymore," Allie said. "Brent Meacham found out and he's telling everyone."

Darcy sighed. "I still don't think you had to lie to us about—"

Two boys crashed into the table, wrestling over a note. "That's mine! I want to give it her!" Brandon Fallow shouted.

"It's about my friend!" Harry Lamont yelled. "I should be the one to tell her!"

The note fell on the table, and Stephanie snatched it up. "Some more juicy news for my column?" she asked happily, dropping it into her book bag.

"Yeah!" both boys answered at once. "But you didn't hear it from us," Brandon added.

"Well, thanks for the tip, guys." She smiled at Brandon. He was one of the cutest boys in school, and here he was, actually passing her a note!

"Stephanie," Darcy started again, "I think you owe Allie and me more of an explanation. You lied to us."

"I didn't really lie," Stephanie said, trying to convince herself as well as them. "I just didn't come right out with all the details." She took a bite of her sandwich as Ron Martinez and Kara Landford walked by.

"Hey, Stephanie," Ron said. "I heard we're getting full-day passes for the Fun City party, and—"

"I've got something really juicy for your column, Stephanie," Kara said, interrupting Ron. "But not here. Call you tonight?"

"Sure!" Stephanie shouted. "I'm always available for a good scoop."

"Stephanie," Darcy said. "I can't believe you couldn't tell *us* your secret. You *know* you can trust us."

The bell rang, and suddenly everyone was jumping up from their tables and jamming trash into the barrels near the doors leading to the hallway.

"Sorry, guys," Stephanie said, scooting back her chair. "Gotta go. I've got major tips to follow up on. See ya 'round!" And she dashed from the cafeteria, fishing in her book bag for the notes people had given her.

She couldn't wait to get started on the next column. If people thought the last one was a winner, she'd really show them what she could do in the next issue!

CHAPTER
4

◆ ◀ ◢ ◆

As Stephanie stepped through the back door on Friday afternoon, the phone was already ringing. "I've got it!" she shouted, throwing herself across the tile floor of the kitchen and sliding to the wall phone.

"Hello?" she gasped into the speaker.

"Hi, is this Stephanie Tanner?"

D.J. walked into the kitchen, munching on an apple. "Hurry up, Steph, I've got to use the phone."

"Yes, this is Stephanie. Who's this?" Stephanie asked.

"It's Lizzie Timmons. When I ran into you in the hall at school, I promised I'd call you tonight."

"Right," Stephanie said, fishing her notebook out of her purse. She couldn't remember if Lizzie had stopped her or not. All week, so many kids had been passing her notes or offering her tips for her column, she couldn't remember anymore who they were. "What's up, Lizzie?"

"Well," Lizzie began, "you can't say you got this from me."

"That information will never pass my lips," Stephanie promised. "All my sources are completely confidential."

D.J. rolled her eyes.

"Okay, then. Here goes. You know that Cheryl Craft has been going with her boyfriend, Tom, like forever?"

"Yeah," Stephanie said, hoping Lizzie had some really hot news she could use for the column.

"I saw Tom with Polly Garcia at the bus stop. And they were acting real chummy, if you know what I mean."

"Tom and Polly?" Stephanie started scribbling notes as fast as she could. "Where was Cheryl?"

"Who knows? I haven't seen her around for ages. Maybe she moved away or something."

"No," Stephanie said thoughtfully, "we'd have heard about that. Tell me exactly what you saw. Were they holding hands or anything like that?''

"Stephanie!" D.J. cried. "You're *spying* on people! That's revolting!"

"Sssssh!" Stephanie waved her away.

D.J. tossed her apple core into the trash can but didn't leave the kitchen.

"Go on, Lizzie. What did you see with your own eyes? I want every detail."

"Well, there wasn't much to see," Lizzie said, sounding less sure of herself. "They weren't exactly holding hands. But, well, maybe they were *touching* hands."

"Huh?"

"It was raining when we left school, remember? Tom and Polly were standing beside each other, and Polly had an umbrella. She invited Tom to step under it with her. She was sort of looking at him funny."

"Sounds serious to me," Stephanie murmured. "Thanks for the tip. I'll see you at school Monday." She hung up and turned around to find D.J. still watching her. "Yes?"

"I've got a message from Dad. He wants you to clean out your corner of the garage this afternoon, before he gets home."

Stephanie groaned. "Why me?"

D.J. laughed. "I already finished my part, and Michelle's done with hers."

"Okay. I might as well get it over with." Stephanie headed for the back door, but the phone rang before she'd touched the knob.

D.J. picked up the receiver. "Tanner residence." There was a pause while she listened. Then she held out the phone to Stephanie. "It's for you. He asked for the newspaper reporter. But hurry up, will you? I've got to make a call."

Stephanie took the phone. "Hello?"

"Hi, Stephanie, this is Ron Martinez. Listen, about the Fun City party . . ."

"Yeah?" Stephanie said.

"I talked to Mr. Assante," he continued, "and he said he doesn't know anything about it. He said the seventh grade doesn't have enough money for that kind of class party. So what's the deal? Are we going or not?"

"Well . . ." Stephanie said, stalling. *Everyone's getting really psyched about this Fun City thing,* she thought. *It's only a rumor!*

"Stephanie!" D.J. didn't bother to whisper this time. "Will you please get off."

Stephanie plugged a finger in her ear. "Listen,

Ron. Sorry, but I'll have to talk to you Monday."
She said good-bye and hung up. She'd have to deal
with the Fun City problem later.

"So, Steph," Danny asked at dinner that night,
"how did the garage turn out?"

Stephanie winced. "I didn't exactly get to it yet,
Dad. Sorry. There were a lot of things I had to take
care of for school."

"Oh. Your teachers loaded you down with
homework for the weekend, huh?" Danny asked.

"Uh, well . . ." Stephanie paused. She hadn't
even thought about her homework.

"The phone's been ringing off the hook with tips
for her column all afternoon," D.J. informed
Danny dryly.

"That's great, honey," Danny said to Stephanie.

"Not really," Michelle said. "The phone rang so
much, I could hardly hear the television."

Danny laughed. "Well, the column's important.
But so's a clean garage. Why don't you do it right
after dinner, Stephanie, and get it out of the way?"

"I'll help you, Steph," Becky offered. "The twins,
too. They love playing with your old toys."

"Great, thanks!" Stephanie said, chewing on a
chicken wing. "I'm really backed up and—"

The phone rang, and both Stephanie and D.J. shoved back their chairs.

Jesse held up his hand. "In the interest of getting through this meal, I'll get it."

Stephanie sat down with a sigh. She hoped whoever was calling could wait for her to finish eating. She started chewing faster.

"Stephanie Tanner's office, may I help you?" Jesse said. "No, we're having dinner now. You can call back after seven o'clock. Fine, good-bye." He hung up.

"You didn't take down a name and phone number?" Stephanie asked.

"No, if it's important enough, they'll call back."

"But if they *don't* and I missed something—"

"Sorry, Steph, but you can't take phone calls during dinner," Danny said.

Stephanie glanced at Jesse, Becky, and Joey, hoping for some support. No one said a word.

The doorbell rang, then the phone almost at the same time.

"I think it's time Stephanie got a private line," Danny said.

"Dad! Do you really mean it?" Stephanie asked.

Danny grinned. "Dream on, honey."

* * *

Stephanie couldn't wait to get back to her gossip column, but the garage came first. She stood by while her father inspected the job she, Becky, and the twins had done.

"You know, maybe I should invest in a wet-dry vacuum." Danny peered closely at the cement floor of the garage. "This floor could use a really good cleaning. But you did a nice job," he commented, rocking back on his heels with his hands in his pockets. "Especially since you were only out here for fifteen minutes."

"Well," Stephanie admitted, "I didn't do as much as everyone else. School stuff . . . you know."

"So Becky ended up doing most of the work?" Danny asked.

"She had Nicky and Alex to help her," Stephanie replied.

Her dad laughed and motioned to the two boys, who had found a ball of twine and were happily unrolling it across the floor as he spoke. "Yeah, they're a big help cleaning up."

Stephanie smiled.

"By the way," Danny said. "While you were out here, I took a call for you. Something about the seventh-grade class party."

"Oh, right," Stephanie said. "Hey, Dad, you said

you did a show on Fun City. Is it as fantastic as everybody says?"

"It's amazing," Danny told her. "I think I can manage to take us all in a few weeks. And I just might do another show on it, maybe next month. Mr. Costello—he's the manager there—says that during the holidays they decorate the place with about nine zillion lights."

It would be great if the class really could have the party there, Stephanie thought. *Much better than the fishpond at the park.*

"Phone, Steph!" D.J.'s voice called from the back door. "Surprise, surprise."

Stephanie pushed the Fun City problem out of her mind and ran for the kitchen.

D.J. handed her the receiver and returned to her homework, which covered the entire kitchen table.

"Hey, Steph!" a voice said. "You'll be famous if you print this! I've got the greatest scoop ever for your column."

Stephanie whipped out her notebook and grabbed a pencil from the message pad by the phone. "What is it?"

"I can't tell you over the phone. Meet me tomorrow morning at the mall. We can talk there. I'll be near the eatery on the fountain side."

"I'll be there!" Stephanie cried excitedly. She'd barely hung up the phone before it was ringing again.

"Give me a break!" D.J. wailed.

"Tanner residence," Stephanie said.

"Hi, Steph, this is Darcy."

"Hey, Darce, what's up?" Stephanie was still finishing her notes from her last call and was only half-listening.

"I just wanted to remind you that we're supposed to meet Allie to go Rollerblading tomorrow," Darcy said.

"Uh-oh," Stephanie said, putting down the pencil.

"Uh-oh? What does that mean?"

"It means, well, I don't exactly have time to go Rollerblading tomorrow. I have a pretty tight schedule for Saturday."

"Wait a minute. You had a schedule that included me and Allie!"

"I know, but things have changed. I have deadlines and I have to meet an important contact at the mall. We can go another time, can't we?" Stephanie said.

Darcy was silent on the other end of the line.

"Darce, you still there?" Stephanie asked.

"Yeah, I'm here."

"I really wanted to do something with you guys tomorrow, but I don't have any choice. Work comes first, right?"

"I guess. Well, call me if you get a chance, okay?"

"Sure, sure, I'll do that," Stephanie promised, but her thoughts were already far away, plotting her next, most spectacular column ever.

CHAPTER
5

♦ ◄ ▪ ♦

Monday at noon, Stephanie walked into the cafeteria for lunch followed by a small mob of kids who ran off to a table against one wall where the *Scribe* staff was selling newspapers. As she was looking to see if Darcy and Allie were already in the cafeteria, a loud voice rang out above the noise. "Hey, Stephanie!"

She spun around, and there was Brenda. The *Scribe* editor was making her way toward her across the crowded lunchroom with a determined look on her face.

"Oh, no," Stephanie murmured.

She'd been avoiding Brenda ever since Brent

Meacham leaked her identity. *Now I'm in trouble,* she thought nervously. *Brenda wanted me to keep it a secret.*

"Stephanie," Brenda said, "I couldn't find you anywhere this morning."

"Sorry, I've been pretty busy."

"Yeah." Brenda took a deep breath. "That's exactly what I want to talk to you about."

Oh, oh, here goes, Stephanie thought.

"I just wanted to tell you what a great job you're doing," Brenda said.

"Huh?"

"You're doing super with the gossip column!"

"You mean, you aren't angry that everyone knows I'm the one writing it?" Stephanie asked.

Brenda rolled her eyes. "Who cares whether they know or not? All that matters is *we sell papers!* We sold out our first printing Friday." She pointed to a table where two newspaper staffers were collecting quarters for copies of the *Scribe.* Only a few remained on the table. "And the second printing is going just as fast."

"Wow!" Stephanie shouted. "You think *my* column did that?"

"Not all of it," Brenda said. "But the gossip column seems to be what everyone's talking about, so maybe it's a big factor. In the next issue we'll print your byline. It's not like it's a secret anymore that you write the column."

"Great!" Stephanie said. "I can't wait to see my name in print."

"Don't forget our meeting after school," Brenda said, and walked away. Stephanie turned around and continued her search for Darcy and Allie. She hadn't seen them all weekend. She wondered if they'd gone Rollerblading without her and felt a pang of regret.

It was just that she'd been so busy tracking down story leads and meeting with kids who said they had exciting gossip. Unfortunately, most of their news was either total lies or too boring to print, so she'd wasted a lot of time. But still, it had been exciting, she thought with a grin. If she wrote something—almost *anything* in her column— everyone who read it believed her.

As she crossed the crowded cafeteria, Stephanie passed a group of kids talking to Mr. Assante. She heard the words Fun City and saw the teacher frown and shake his head. *Uh-oh*, she thought. So many kids thought the class really was having its party at the amusement park. And by now Mr. Assante had to know she wrote the gossip column.

He might even be mad because she'd started the rumor. She'd better avoid him for a while, until she figured out a way to explain things.

When Stephanie finally reached the table she usually shared with Darcy and Allie, she saw that her friends were already there, halfway through their lunches.

"Finally!" Allie cried, brushing her soft brown hair out of her eyes. "We thought we'd never see you again."

"Sorry, guys," Stephanie said. "I've just been a little tied up."

Allie made a face. "A little?"

"Hey, I have to do my job, don't I?"

"Sure," Allie admitted. She glanced up as two boys passed their table, carrying lunch trays. "Oh, wow," she murmured.

Stephanie followed her glance and saw Brandon Fallow and Adam Green. Allie had always thought Adam was the greatest-looking guy in their class.

"Hey, Allie, why don't you just stamp Adam's name on your forehead and let everyone know," Darcy teased.

Allie elbowed her friend. "You should talk. You could hardly stay in your seat when Jerry Wilkes walked by a few minutes ago."

45

Stephanie's ears pricked up. "Jerry Wilkes?" She looked at Darcy in amazement. "You like *Jerry?*"

Darcy shrugged. "I don't know . . . maybe."

"Maybe?" Allie prodded. "Like, how much is maybe?"

Darcy squirmed uncomfortably on her chair. "I don't know; a little, I guess. Everyone thinks he's a brainiac and kind of geeky, but I think he's nice."

"Well, he isn't exactly your type," Stephanie said. "Is he?"

"I've know for a long time that Jerry has a crush on you, Darcy," Allie said. "After all, he did get caught passing that note to you in social studies last week. But, well, I never thought in a million years that you liked him too."

Darcy nibbled nervously at her tuna sandwich. "It's no big deal. He helps me with my math homework sometimes. He's really smart."

"He does get good grades," Stephanie pointed out. "I'll bet he aces every math test."

"He's more than smart," Darcy admitted. "He's funny and a lot more mature than most seventh-grade boys." Her eyes lit up. "Did you know he has his own set of drums in his basement? He plays them along with his CDs!"

Stephanie and Allie exchanged surprised glances.

"You've been in Jerry's basement?" Allie asked.

"Well, n-no," Darcy stammered. "Of course not. He just told me about them." She looked around the cafeteria uncomfortably, then changed the subject. "Let's walk home today. It's supposed to be really nice this afternoon."

"Sure," Allie said. "That will give us time to talk"—she glanced meaningfully at Stephanie—"since we didn't get together *all weekend.*"

"Um, I can't," Stephanie said. "Got a meeting at the newspaper office right after school. We'll have—"

"We know!" Allie groaned. "We'll have to *reschedule.*"

Stephanie sat in the newspaper office, finishing off her latest batch of stories. With a final few pecks at the keyboard of the computer and a sigh of satisfaction, she printed up her copy. With her story in hand, Stephanie jumped to her feet and rushed up to Brenda's desk at the front of the room.

"Here it is!" she said grandly. "My best column yet! I'm outta here!"

"Hold it!" Brenda shouted. "I have to look this over before you go."

"What for? Everyone seems to like my stories." Stephanie had been thinking as she finished off her column that she might still have time to catch up with Darcy and Allie.

Brenda glanced down the lines on the page, then flipped to the second one, reading quickly. She turned them over and frowned. "Is this it? Only three stories?"

Stephanie shrugged. "They're good ones. Next time, maybe I'll have more."

"Sorry, Steph," Brenda said sternly. "I need another item to fill space. Write me one more, and make it fast. I want to lock up the office and get out of here myself."

Stephanie swallowed hard and dragged herself back to her desk. Another story? There weren't any other stories.

She opened her notebook and flipped through. Tons of kids had given her so-called stories. But most of them weren't interesting enough.

Stephanie sighed. What was she going to do?

She looked up at the clock, then at Brenda, who was busily clearing her desk. Stephanie racked her brains.

Nothing.

Then she remembered her conversation with

Allie and Darcy in the cafeteria. About Darcy's crush on Jerry. That was a true story! But could she print it?

"Move it, Tanner!" Brenda bellowed, plodding toward her down the aisle. "Hand over that last item!"

"All right, all right!"

Stephanie began writing as fast as she could: *Rumor has it, a certain nerdy guy has a crush on a certain gorgeous, cool girl in homeroom L–R. By the way, readers, this guy might really be crazy about her. He got caught passing love notes to her in social studies!*

"There!" she said shakily, handing the last page to Brenda.

Brenda stuffed the sheet into her folder. "Good, we can enter this in the computer as soon as I've edited it."

Stephanie glanced up at the clock. It was almost four. There was no hope of catching Darcy and Allie now.

She walked alone through the deserted corridors and took the side door across the parking lot. As she went, she worried about this latest column. The other stories were basically harmless, but what about the one on Darcy and Jerry?

She'd done her best to keep their identities secret. She hadn't even used initials, and there were at least twenty-five kids in Darcy's homeroom, with more girls than boys. People probably wouldn't even know who she was talking about.

And anyway, who would suspect Darcy had a crush on somebody like Jerry Wilkes?

Stephanie sighed. Maybe it would be all right after all. Still, a little flutter in her stomach told her she had good reason to worry.

CHAPTER

6

◆ ▼ ◆ ◆

On Friday, Stephanie couldn't wait until the end of the day.

"The paper should be out by last period," Brenda had told her.

Stephanie suspected everyone in the school would snatch them up, just like before.

When the dismissal bell rang, Stephanie raced out of class all the way to the cafeteria. She grabbed one of the first copies from the stack and held out a quarter to the ninth grader selling them.

"You don't have to pay, Steph," the girl said, smiling at her. "You're on the staff."

Stephanie grinned. *Totally amazing*, she thought. *Even a ninth grader knows who I am.*

She flipped through until she found the Secret's Out column. This week she even had her own by-line! Stephanie Tanner!

Her eyes drifted down the column as she checked out each item. They were just as she'd written them, even the bit about Darcy and Jerry—only the part about Jerry passing the note had been left out. There hadn't been enough space on the page to fit it in.

"I guess Brenda had to cut some lines," she murmured to herself.

It was just as well. This way there would be fewer clues for people to guess the identity of the girl and boy in the story.

As Stephanie started down the hall, she saw Mr. Assante at the other end. Two kids were with him.

"I keep telling everyone the Fun City party is just a rumor," Mr. Assante was saying.

Stephanie did a quick about-face and turned the corner. She didn't want to face Mr. Assante yet. She hadn't even tried to figure out what to say to him. She took another route to the gym and saw Allie and Darcy at their meeting spot by the pay phone. Her two friends were talking quietly, their heads together. As soon as they spotted Stephanie they moved apart.

"What's up?" Stephanie asked.

"Nothing," Darcy said coolly. "Nothing important anyway."

Allie changed the subject. "So, what are we going to do this weekend?"

Stephanie was tired of newspaper work. It was all she'd been thinking about for days, and she was beginning to miss hanging out with Darcy and Allie. "How about we go to the mall on Saturday?" she suggested.

"And do what?" Darcy asked glumly. She started walking, and the other two girls fell into step with her.

"We'll do what we always do," Stephanie said. "Check out the cool clothes and jewelry. I want to shop for some new scrunchies and bow clips for my hair."

Allie nodded encouragingly at Darcy. "And there's a new Keanu Reeves movie at the theater. We can see it on Sunday. My mom will drive us to the movie if your dad drives us on Saturday, Steph."

"Sounds great!" Stephanie said, swinging her book bag over one shoulder. It really would be nice to spend some time with her friends.

"I guess," Darcy said, a little coolly.

Stephanie stared at her. "What's wrong with you?" She had a feeling she knew, but she didn't want to be the one to bring it up.

"Not a thing. Why would anything be wrong?" Darcy said, her dark eyes flashing. She started walking faster. "I'll just have to see if I can make it to the mall tomorrow. I have a lot planned."

"Like what?" Stephanie asked.

"Things," Darcy said vaguely. "Call me tomorrow morning. I should know by then if I can go."

Stephanie didn't push her any further. She had a feeling she might not like what Darcy would say if she got her talking.

On Saturday morning, Stephanie marched across the kitchen, grabbed a piece of toast off the plate on the counter, and reached for the telephone.

"Starting awfully early, aren't you?" Becky asked. She was seated at the kitchen table, eating with the twins.

"I'm going to the mall today with Allie and Darcy. Dad says he'll drive us over, then pick us up around two in the afternoon."

"Sounds like fun. But Joey's driving me and the twins over to the mall, and Michelle's coming too. Why don't you girls just join us? The more the merrier!"

"Great!" Stephanie said. "I could tell Dad wasn't really into chauffeuring us around anyway. He rented this new wet-dry vacuum. I think he's going to try to sterilize the garage." She picked up the receiver and dialed Darcy's number.

The phone rang five times before anyone picked it up.

"Hello?" a voice finally said from the other end. It didn't sound like Darcy.

"Darce, is that you?" Stephanie asked hesitantly.

"Yeah, who did you think it would be?"

Stephanie winced at Darcy's unfriendly tone. "I don't know . . . I just . . . Never mind. I'm calling about the mall. Okay if we pick you up in about an hour?"

There was silence from the other end.

"I asked if it's okay if—"

"I heard you," Darcy said hurriedly. "Look, I'm really busy today, so I think I'll pass on the mall."

"You don't want to go?" Stephanie couldn't believe her ears. Darcy loved shopping at the mall. She loved it even more than *she*, Stephanie Tanner, did!

"I said, I'm busy," Darcy repeated.

Stephanie hated the way Darcy was acting. She had to find out what was wrong.

"Listen, you're not mad at me or anything, are you?"

"Why should I be mad at you?" Darcy asked tightly.

Stephanie groaned into the phone. "I don't know . . . maybe the column?"

There, she'd said it right out. Darcy had to talk to her now.

"You mean the one where you said Jerry Wilkes has a crush on me?"

Stephanie swallowed and gripped the receiver tighter. "Yeah, that one."

"I don't see why that should make me mad," Darcy said calmly. "After all, why should it matter if some nerd has a crush on me or not?"

"But—" Stephanie began.

"I mean," Darcy broke in, "it's not as if I really *like* him or anything like that! I just borrow his math homework once in a while. It's nothing serious; we're just study partners."

Stephanie was about to point out that on Monday, Darcy had said she really liked Jerry because he was smart, funny, and mature. But she figured it wouldn't be a good move, under the circumstances.

"So you're sure you don't want to come with us?" Stephanie asked one last time.

"Yeah," Darcy said softly. "I'll catch you guys later." And she hung up.

The Tanners picked up Allie at ten o'clock, and in less than fifteen minutes the group arrived at the mall. Crammed into the car with Becky, Joey, the twins, and Michelle, Stephanie and Allie didn't have much opportunity for a private conversation. Stephanie was dying to ask her if she knew what was really wrong with Darcy.

As soon as they stepped into the mall and the others took off in their own direction, Stephanie pulled Allie aside.

"When I called Darcy this morning, she was acting really strange," Stephanie said. "Any idea why?"

Allie looked around as if her mind was already on shopping. "Not really," she mumbled.

Stephanie squinted at her suspiciously. She was sure Allie did know something. She was determined to get it out of her before they went home today.

They window-shopped for over an hour, even trying on some skirts and tops at a store that was having a sale. Stephanie had a little money saved up, and she could have bought one of the outfits at the sale price, but her heart wasn't into finding bargains that day.

"I don't know; it's just not the same without Darcy here." She sighed, licking the icing off a gigantic cinnamon bun she'd bought at one of the food shops.

"Yeah," Allie agreed.

Stephanie stopped and stared at her. "You know what's going on with her, don't you?"

Allie tipped her head to one side and pretended to check out the price tag on a sweater in a window they were passing. "Why would I know anything more than you do about Darcy?"

Stephanie groaned out loud. "I don't believe you two! Why are you being so mean to me?"

"*Mean?*" Allie asked, stopping to face her. "I don't think we're the ones being mean."

"What have I done that's mean?" Stephanie supposed she knew what Allie would say, but she had to hear the words.

"Look," Allie said reluctantly, "I promised Darcy I wouldn't say anything to you. She doesn't want to make a big deal about this, but . . ."

"Well?"

Allie popped the last bite of her bagel into her mouth and licked her fingers. "I talked to Darcy yesterday after school and again early this morning. She's really upset over this Jerry thing."

"Is that all?" Stephanie asked.

"Is that *all?*" Allie echoed. "I think it's a whole lot. I don't think it was very nice to you to print that story about her."

Stephanie hated to see the angry look in Allie's eyes. "But no one would ever think Darcy was interested in someone as geeky as Jerry. No one will guess who it's about," she objected.

"A few already have," Allie said. "Lizzie Timmons called her last night to ask if it was true about her and Jerry."

"Oh," Stephanie said, biting her lip.

"Besides, that's not the point. Darcy told you about Jerry because she trusted you. She thought you'd keep personal stuff like that to yourself."

Stephanie stared at the tips of her sneakers. Her stomach felt totally hollow, even though she'd just finished the enormous sweet roll. Now she was so upset, she didn't even remember how it had tasted.

"But I had a really tight deadline," she objected. "I had to come up with *something!*"

Allie wouldn't look at her. "You still shouldn't have let Darcy down like that."

All the way home from the mall, Stephanie was

miserable. Allie hardly said a word to her in the car. Stephanie could only hope that the next day, when the girls all went to the movies together, she could find a way to make it up to Darcy so they could be best friends again. And then maybe Allie wouldn't be angry, too.

On Sunday morning, Stephanie took some extra money out of her piggy bank, deciding she'd treat Darcy and Allie to popcorn and sodas.

As she was combing her hair and tying on a ribbon that matched her pink-and-gray outfit, the phone rang.

D.J. answered it in her room. "It's for you, Steph! Make it fast—I have to call Kimmy."

"Why does D.J. only have to use the phone when I'm on it?" Stephanie muttered as she ran to pick up the phone. Maybe it was someone from school with a really good tip for her column. She needed ideas badly. Good stories were getting a lot harder to come by.

"Hello?" she said into the phone.

"Hi, Steph, this is Allie."

"Hey, Allie, I'm glad you called!" Stephanie was so glad that Allie was still talking to her. Maybe she could ask her opinion about apologizing to Darcy at the theater.

"I just wanted to let you know, Darcy and I won't be going to the movies with you," Allie said.

Stephanie felt like she'd been hit in the stomach with a soccer ball. "What?" she gasped.

"I just talked to Darcy. She's not feeling too well. Neither am I."

"But maybe you'd both feel better if you went to the movies," Stephanie suggested.

"No, I don't think so," Allie said. "Talk to you later . . ."

Stephanie slowly hung up the phone. She closed her eyes and thought about what had happened between her, Allie, and Darcy. She and Allie had been best friends for so long. And Darcy, too. Maybe Allie was right about the article about Darcy. Maybe she had gone too far with this whole gossip column thing.

"Stephie! Stephie!" two voices rang through the house.

With a sigh, Stephanie walked out of D.J.'s room and closed the door behind her. She found Nicky and Alex in the living room with Aunt Becky.

"What is it, guys?" she asked glumly.

"We got a present for you!" Alex cried, holding up a brown paper bag.

Stephanie took the bag from him, trying to look pleased.

"It's okay to open it," Becky said, laughing. "It's not a dead frog or a snake or anything."

Stephanie stuck her hand inside, felt something like a hat, and pulled it out.

It was a baseball cap. On the front, over the brim, were the words *Fun City*, stitched in neon pink thread.

"Mr. Costello, the manager, sent the caps to the twins," Becky explained. "But they're too big, so Nicky and Alex gave one to D.J. This one's for you."

"Thanks a lot, guys. It's perfect." Stephanie stuck the cap on her head and tried to smile. But she felt worse than ever as she thought of all the excitement in school over the Fun City rumor she'd started.

Now she had two major problems: Darcy and Fun City. And she didn't have any idea how to solve either one of them.

CHAPTER
7

◆ ◀ ◆ ◆

Stephanie waited at the telephone outside the gym on Monday morning, but neither Allie nor Darcy showed up. When the first bell rang, signaling that students had ten minutes to get to their homerooms, Stephanie gave up.

She'd planned to get to school early to apologize to Darcy for the item about her and Jerry in her column, but she was beginning to wonder if Darcy would even listen to her. She'd never known Darcy to hold a grudge like this.

There was one other place she could look for Darcy before class. Her locker. Stephanie raced down the hall, skidded around the corner, narrowly missing two eighth-grade boys from the football team, and finally made it to a long row of lockers. Darcy was standing with Allie, pulling out some books.

Stephanie ran up to them. "Hi, guys!" She tried to sound like her usual cheerful self.

Allie turned to her. "Hi, Steph," she said.

Stephanie looked at Darcy. "Listen, Darce, I just wanted to tell you how sorry I am for printing that thing about you. I mean, I guess I just got carried away, looking for cool stories."

Darcy finally faced her. "I guess you did get carried away."

"Yeah, well, I really am sorry," Stephanie said. "I shouldn't have gotten so wrapped up in what I was doing. I didn't think about your feelings."

Darcy studied her expression. "You mean it?"

"Sure. You know I wouldn't do anything to hurt you, not on purpose!"

Allie stepped forward. "I don't think she would, Darcy. I think it was just a bad decision."

"Exactly," Stephanie said, glad that Allie was at last on her side. "I just wasn't thinking straight. I hope you can forgive me."

"Well," Darcy said. "I don't know . . . I'll have to think about it, Stephanie. I mean, it might be a while before I can trust you again, you know."

Stephanie started to say something, but before she could, Brenda came rushing up. "I thought you'd like to know, star writer, all the copies of the paper were snapped up so fast on Friday, we've had to do yet another printing," she said. "We'll distribute it this afternoon sometime."

Stephanie threw a look in Allie and Darcy's direction. Both of her friends were scowling at Brenda.

"Uh, that's great," Stephanie said, trying not to sound too enthusiastic, although she was thrilled with the news.

"Isn't it?" Brenda asked, patting Stephanie on the back. "Well, keep up the good work, Steph. We need lots of juicy stories."

"No problem," Stephanie called after her. "I've got a million of 'em!"

Darcy slammed her locker door shut and fixed Stephanie with a look that could kill.

Stephanie started to say something again, something that would smooth things out with Darcy, but just then Mr. Assante came around the corner. "Ah, Stephanie," he said. "You're just the person I've been looking for. Got a minute to talk?"

"Uh, well . . ." Stephanie swallowed. She was pretty sure she knew what he wanted to talk to her about. "I've got to get to homeroom."

"I'll walk with you," the teacher said. "We can talk on the way."

Stephanie felt trapped, but there was no way out. Giving Allie and Darcy a wave, she headed down the hall with Mr. Assante. "Listen, Mr. Assante, I know what you want to talk about," she told him. "Fun City, right?"

"Bingo," he said. "Ever since that story came out in the paper, I've been bombarded with questions about the class party. Unfortunately, I don't have any answers."

"I know," Stephanie said with a sigh. "I didn't check out my information, which turned out to be all wrong." She took a breath. "But listen, isn't there some way we really could have the class party there? My dad says it's just fantastic."

"I'm sure it is," Mr. Assante said. "There's the small problem of money, though. The class treasury doesn't have enough to cover tickets for eighty-seven students. Admission is ten dollars apiece, and then there's the cost of food. We've budgeted only five dollars per student for the party. That's all we have to spend."

"Maybe there's some way we can earn the difference," Stephanie suggested.

"Four hundred and thirty-five dollars?" Mr. Assante shook his head. "The party is next month. There simply isn't enough time to earn that kind of money."

Stephanie sighed again. "I should never have written that story. I'm really sorry."

"It's not me you should apologize to," Mr. Assante said. "It's all the kids who got their hopes up. Next time, you should check your source. Well, maybe if the student council starts planning now, we can go to Fun City next year." He smiled, but it didn't make Stephanie feel any better.

At least Mr. Assante hadn't been mean about it, she thought as she walked into homeroom. But she couldn't help feeling that she'd let the entire seventh-grade class down by writing that stupid rumor.

It was raining by the time school let out. To make matters worse, Stephanie's bus had broken down. Most of the kids decided to walk instead of waiting for another bus.

Luckily, Stephanie had remembered to bring an umbrella. It happened to be one of Joey's goofy golf umbrellas, and it was big enough to cover a good-sized elephant.

She spotted Darcy and Allie in front of her on the sidewalk. They were walking hunched over, trying to keep their hair from getting wet by holding notebooks over their heads.

"Hey, wait up!" Stephanie called.

She raced up and held the umbrella over them.

"Thanks," Allie mumbled grimly. "This sure is crummy weather."

"That's the biggest umbrella I've ever seen," Darcy remarked reluctantly, as if she couldn't help getting in on the conversation. "Do you take this with you to the beach in the summer?"

Stephanie smiled. "It is pretty big. But it sure comes in handy on a day like this."

The rain seemed to come down even harder as they walked. On the other side of the street was another group of kids, screaming and shouting as the rain pelted down. One of the boys was stomping in every puddle, splashing the girls in his group. Up ahead, another boy walked all by himself. Stephanie squinted through the gray sheets of rain. It was Jerry Wilkes.

She glanced at Darcy and saw that she was looking at him too.

A car whizzed past them and, as luck would have it, sprayed a wave of water from under its tires all over Jerry. He leaped back from the road and shook himself off like a big dog.

"What a g—" Stephanie started to call him a geek, then realized it might not be a good idea in front of Darcy. "Um, I mean, what a shame. Jerry got all wet."

Jerry turned to look back at the kids in the other group. They were hooting at him and shouting rude names. His eyes shifted to the opposite side of the road, and he spotted Darcy. A big grin spread across his face.

"Here comes Jerry," Stephanie heard Allie whisper to Darcy. "What are you going to do?"

Darcy clamped her teeth down on her lower lip.

Jerry ran up to the three girls, but his eyes were fixed only on Darcy. "Hey, Darcy, haven't seen you around much."

"I, uh, I know." She struggled with the words. "I've sort of been busy."

He nodded, still grinning widely. His eyeglasses were covered with raindrops and looked useless. "I have a great idea," he said. "Why don't you come over to my house to study tonight, instead of going to the library?"

Darcy's cheeks flushed. She darted a look at Allie, then at Stephanie. "I, um . . . I can't. I mean, I'm real, real busy . . . and I have to help my mom paint the living room."

"Well, what about tomorrow after school?" Jerry asked. "We have that math quiz coming up. Don't you want to study together for it?"

"I told you," Darcy said stiffly, "I can't. In fact, I won't have time to meet with you for a while . . . for a long while." She started to turn away, but Jerry put out his hand and stopped her.

"What's wrong, Darcy? You're acting weird."

"Nothing's wrong!" she insisted. "I just have a lot of other things to do . . . things that are more important."

Jerry looked hurt, and Stephanie felt awful. She knew Darcy was acting this way because she and Allie were there, watching.

Darcy hurried away, and Stephanie had to run to keep up with her and hold the umbrella over her head. As she looked back she could see Jerry standing in the rain, looking totally miserable.

"You didn't have to do that," Stephanie said

softly, feeling terrible for breaking up Darcy and Jerry's friendship.

"Don't tell me what I didn't have to do," Darcy snapped, avoiding Stephanie's eyes. "I've got to get home."

And she took off down the street at a run.

CHAPTER
8

◆ ◄ ▪ ◆

Allie and Stephanie walked on together in silence while the rain came down harder and harder. Stephanie felt awful. How could she have done this to one of her best friends ever?

At last she broke the silence. "I don't think Darcy will ever speak to me again," she said.

"It'll be all right. Just give her time," Allie said softly.

Stephanie brushed tears from her eyes. "I didn't mean to hurt her like this. Will you tell her I'm sorry?" she asked. "I'm afraid she'll hang up on me if I try to call her."

Allie took a long while to think about that. "You really mean it? You are sorry?"

"Sure, I am."

"Okay, I'll tell her," Allie said. "But Steph, you can't just keep on writing those awful stories about people and hurting their feelings."

"I know," Stephanie said. But deep down she didn't want to lose the gossip column job. It was really fun. There had to be a way to keep writing it without messing up friendships and making people believe stuff that wasn't true. "Listen, I don't want to quit my job with the newspaper," she said. "But I promise to tone down my articles." She suddenly had a super idea. "Hey, why don't you help me come up with new ideas for The Secret's Out?"

"Me?" Allie asked. "I don't have any great stories."

"Maybe you don't think you do, but you know practically everyone in the whole school. I bet we can come up with some interesting stuff. And if I write anything too wild, you can just tell me!"

"All right," Allie agreed. "Where do we work? My house or yours?"

"Let's go to my dad's study. I can use his word processor."

They arrived at the Tanner house to find Michelle playing with two of her friends in the living room. They had Barbie clothes spread all across the floor.

"We're setting up a Barbie clothes swap," Michelle explained to Stephanie and Allie. "I've invited three other girls to bring over their clothes, then we'll trade for outfits we'd like to have."

Stephanie smiled. "Does dad know you're going into business in our house?"

Michelle nodded seriously. "Sure."

Just then, Joey walked into the living room. When he saw he had an audience, he grinned. "Hey, guys, I've got a great one: How do you keep an elephant from charging?"

"I give up," Allie said.

"You take away his credit card!"

Stephanie let out a large moan, but Allie laughed. She hadn't heard the joke as many times as Stephanie had.

After milk and cookies in the kitchen, Stephanie and Allie went up to D.J.'s room.

They sat in silence for a few moments, looking at each other.

"Got anything yet?" Stephanie asked.

"Not really," Allie admitted. "You know, this is harder than I thought it would be. All I can come up with is stuff like the change in the cafeteria menu."

"What change?" Stephanie asked, her hopes rising.

"I heard that starting in two weeks we'll be able to get pizza every day, not just on Fridays."

"Really?" Stephanie asked.

"Yeah. I heard one of the women who works in the food service line talking to the cashier, so it comes from a reliable source."

"Great!" Stephanie started typing. "What else?"

"Well . . ." Allie began slowly. "I think I heard something about the girls' field hockey captain moving."

"That's Anna Birch. She's in ninth grade."

"Right. Anyway, there's a big tournament between six schools next month, and it sounds like she may be gone by then."

"This is super," Stephanie said, typing away. "John Muir's winning field hockey team will lose its captain. Will they be able to pull through and score without her?"

"I love it!" Allie cried, smiling for the first time all day. "See, you can write good stuff about people that won't hurt their feelings."

"Well, it's not as exciting as some of my other stories," Stephanie said, then she saw the disapproving expression on Allie's face. "But you're right. It's a lot safer."

"How many more do we need?" Allie asked.

"Probably two, but we might be able to get along on just one more good one," Stephanie said.

After ten minutes of silence, Allie said, "I can't think of a thing."

"Someone told me that Tom Andrews was with Polly Garcia last week, and they were looking really cozy," Stephanie said, watching Allie's expression.

"I don't know about that one," Allie said, frowning. "He and Cheryl Craft have been going together for a long time. Are you sure about your facts?"

"Well, it's just a rumor, but it would sure make a good story."

"It's chancy. But I haven't seen Cheryl around lately. Maybe she ditched Tom?"

"Well, I can't say that because I don't know for sure," Stephanie admitted. "But I do know that Tom and Polly were together at the bus stop, sharing an umbrella and standing super-close."

Allie sighed. "If we can't come up with something else, that will have to do."

"After all," Stephanie crowed, typing out her last story, "news is news!"

*   *   *

After Allie left, Stephanie retyped her stories neatly. As she was straightening up D.J.'s room, her father walked in.

"Looks like someone's been working hard," he said, smiling at her. "Are you all finished?"

"Yup," she said, waving the pages of her column. "Hey, Dad, there was something I wanted to ask you about."

He put down his briefcase and blew imaginary dust off the top of his computer. "What's that, Steph?"

"Sometimes don't places like Fun City give you stuff because you're a celebrity? You know, like Michelle's cup?"

"Sometimes," he said. "Why?"

"Well, I thought maybe you could get me some free day passes for Fun City."

"But I'm taking us all there Saturday," Danny said.

"I know, but I didn't say the passes would be for *us*. I want them for my class at school." Stephanie took a deep breath, then plunged on. "See, I sort of said in my column that our class party was going to be at Fun City this year. But I have a feeling that would be too expensive, so I thought you could—"

"Whoa, whoa, whoa," said her father, holding up his hands as if he was waving off a charging bull. "How many kids are in your class?"

"Give or take a few ..." Stephanie said weakly, "about eighty-seven."

Danny laughed. "You want me to get free tickets for a whole day at Fun City for eighty-seven kids?"

"I guess you'd better add a few for chaperones," Stephanie said helpfully.

"I'm sorry, honey, but that's just not possible."

"But I need to find a way to get my class to Fun City," Stephanie said. "I put it in my column, and I didn't think anyone would take a rumor like that seriously. But they did! I can't disappoint the whole seventh grade!"

Danny sighed. "I guess this turned into a much bigger deal than you'd planned. Sort of like the time Michelle used half a box of detergent in the washing machine."

"It's worse than that," Stephanie said. "I mean, Mr. Assante was pretty nice about it, but I could tell he was disappointed in me. And all the kids are going to hate me!"

"Well, have you thought about printing a retraction in your next issue?" Danny said. "That will let everyone know the story's not true, and from then on you'll just do the job right.''

Stephanie swallowed the lump that had suddenly swelled up in her throat. Brenda probably wouldn't agree to printing an admission that the *Scribe* had made a mistake. Besides, that wouldn't get the seventh grade to Fun City.

"Hey, Dad . . . Steph!" Michelle called out as she ran into the room. "Look what Aunt Becky brought me from the TV station!"

Stephanie turned around. Michelle was wearing a new, hot pink T-shirt. On the front was a picture of an enormous roller coaster. Over it in swirly print were the words: *Fun City, the One Place to Be!*

Stephanie groaned. Fun City was the one place her class would never be, unless she figured out a way to get them there.

CHAPTER
9

◆ ◀ ◆ ◆

Thursday morning, Stephanie stood by the pay phone outside the gym, hoping that Allie and Darcy would meet her there. As the minutes ticked past and more kids swarmed into the building, she began to give up hope.

Then, as she was about to leave, she spotted Allie's navy blue scarf and Darcy's red beret weaving through the crowd. "Hey, guys! Over here!" she shouted.

Darcy glanced in her direction, then looked away. She murmured something to Allie and turned down the corridor toward her locker.

Allie walked over to Stephanie.

"Where's Darcy going?" Stephanie asked.

"She said she had to do something before home-room," Allie explained, sounding unsure.

"She's still avoiding me, isn't she?" Stephanie asked. "Didn't you talk to her?"

Allie nodded solemnly. "Yeah. But she says she'll have to wait and see if you keep your word about changing your ways."

"But I really, really am sorry!" Stephanie wailed.

"I know you are," Allie said sympathetically. "Like I said, though, it's just going to take time for Darcy to get over this. Her feelings are hurt."

Stephanie sighed and hoisted her book bag over one shoulder. "Come on, we might as well go to homeroom."

As they walked Stephanie tried to think of things she could do to win back Darcy's trust. "Maybe I could have a sleepover at my house next week-end," she thought out loud. "Just you, me, and Darcy—like old times."

"I don't know," Allie said doubtfully. "Do you think she'd come?"

"I could ask Becky to help me bake Darcy's fa-vorite kind of cake—devil's food, with fudge frost-ing." Stephanie was beginning to feel hopeful again. "Yeah, and we could rent a bunch of videos and watch movies all night long."

Allie smiled. "I have to admit, a night like that would be hard for Darcy to pass up."

They rounded the corner. At the end of the crowded hallway, Stephanie could see Darcy pulling books out of her locker. As she stepped back to close it, Stephanie spotted Jerry heading Darcy's way.

"Oh, look." Stephanie nudged Allie with her elbow.

Allie stopped and squinted into the distance. "Jerry . . . and Darcy. Maybe he'll say something to make her feel better."

"I hope," Stephanie said, crossing her fingers.

As the girls watched, Jerry stared at Darcy and Darcy stared at Jerry. But then Jerry ducked his head and crossed over to the other side of the hall. Darcy spun back to face her locker, and she kept her head buried inside it until he'd passed.

Stephanie released the breath she'd been holding. "I can't believe it. They both look so miserable. They won't even talk to each other."

"It's awful," Allie murmured.

Stephanie felt a guilty twinge in her stomach. "I've really messed things up for her." She felt worse than ever.

The day passed in a gray blur. Stephanie

couldn't concentrate on her classes. She didn't even have any fun playing soccer, which she loved, because a bunch of kids asked her about the class party. She didn't have the nerve to tell them they might not be going to Fun City, but she couldn't exactly say they *were* going, either.

Halfway through the afternoon, she was walking to math class when Tanya Monroe, a ninth-grade girl on the newspaper staff, stopped her in the hall. "Hey, Steph, remember the new issue comes out today. Look for my article in it." The paper usually came out on Fridays, but it was a special early edition announcing the student council election.

"Sure," Stephanie said without enthusiasm.

"It's pretty good, if I do say so myself," Tanya said, smiling shyly. "I mean, it's not as cool as the stuff you put in your gossip column, but I think I did a good job writing about the teacher of the week, Mr. Assante."

"I'm sure you did," Stephanie said, trying to be polite.

"Would you like an advance copy?" Tanya asked. She juggled her books and pulled out a newspaper. "I picked up two just as they came off the press. They won't be distributed until the end of the day, but Brenda said I could have these."

"Fine," Stephanie murmured. "That's nice of you."

"Well, I'll see you at the next staff meeting," Tanya said cheerfully.

Stephanie started off down the hall again. She was suddenly aware that there were fewer kids in the hall now. The bell would ring any minute. She'd better hurry.

Still, she couldn't resist the temptation to take a quick peek at her own column. Maybe the thrill of seeing her name in print again would cheer her up.

She flipped to the third page and glanced down the columns. There it was, "The Secret's Out, by Stephanie Tanner." She drew in a deep breath and smiled. A year ago, she never would have imagined having her own column in the *Scribe*. Now it was the one part of the paper that every kid at school read first. Some had even told her that The Secret's Out was the only reason they bought the paper!

She felt a flush of pride, then her eyes dropped to the items she'd written. There was the one about the field hockey captain, and the one about the pizza. She felt a little less easy when she read the item about Tom and Polly. However, that was the one she'd needed to give the column at least a little spice.

Then Stephanie saw that there was one more paragraph.

For a moment she thought there had been a misprint, because she'd submitted only three items to Brenda. Then, as she read on, a jolt of horror raced through her.

She stopped dead in the hallway. "Oh, no!" she gasped.

The paragraph read: *Certain nerdy guy mentioned in earlier column was caught passing a note in social studies class to popular girl he's got a massive crush on.*

"Oh, no!" she gasped again. How had *that* gotten into this new issue?

Stephanie's mind raced, and she felt sicker and sicker by the moment. Brenda had added the line they didn't have room for in the last paper. She must have needed something more to fill space!

The bell rang, and Stephanie looked up to find the halls were empty. She felt numb and dizzy and at a loss for what to do. How was she ever going to win back Darcy's trust after she saw this?

All during math, Stephanie tried to think of what she could do to make her latest disaster less of a disaster. Maybe she could somehow keep Darcy from reading the newspaper. She could tell her it was a boring issue and not to waste her time. She could follow her around and distract her so that she wouldn't have time to even think about reading it.

But by the end of the period, Stephanie admitted to herself that nothing she'd come up with so far was likely to work.

She stalked out of math class and shoved her way through the mob of kids in the hall, still trying to figure out what she could do to keep Darcy from seeing the column, when someone grabbed her by the sleeve of her sweater.

When she spun around, it was Cheryl Craft. Tears glittered in Cheryl's eyes.

"What's wrong?" Stephanie started to ask, then remembered her column and closed her mouth.

"You know what's wr-wrong," Cheryl sputtered. "Brenda told me about Tom, and I just couldn't believe it . . . then she showed me your column in the *Scribe.*"

Stephanie swallowed over the lump in her throat. "Gee, Cheryl, I sort of thought you and Tom had broken up. I didn't think it would really matter to you. No one had seen you around with him for a long time."

"I've been out of school for two weeks with a bad case of the flu," Cheryl choked out. "I haven't been around *anyone!*"

"Oh," Stephanie said meekly.

"What I want to know is how you got the news about him and Polly Garcia."

"Well," Stephanie said cautiously, "a reliable source saw them together."

"Where?" Cheryl demanded. "What were they doing? Kissing?"

"Well, no—"

"Holding hands?"

"Not really," Stephanie admitted. "It was more like they were waiting for the bus and sharing an umbrella."

Cheryl stared at her. "Well, there must have been been more to it than that!"

"I'm sure Polly was just being nice to Tom, giving him a place to stand out of the rain," Stephanie said quickly, wanting to downplay the whole incident so that Cheryl would feel better.

"Then why did you write about them in your column?" Cheryl hissed. "Even if you use initials, everyone can guess who you're talking about. You must know something you're not telling me!"

With tears rolling down her cheeks, Cheryl

turned on her heel and stormed off down the hall.

Stephanie stood in the middle of the crush of kids, waiting for her knees to stop shaking. She was close to tears herself.

What have I done? she asked herself. First she'd blown her friendship with Darcy. Now she'd upset Cheryl. Cheryl and Tom had been going together forever . . . like since the beginning of the school year!

There had to be something she could do to set things right.

Stephanie started running down the hall, weaving between students, heading for the media center. That was where the newspaper was being printed, right this very minute. Maybe there was still some way to stop the presses!

CHAPTER
10

◆ ◀ ◆ ◆

Stephanie burst through the door to the media center, gasping for breath. Students had only five minutes between classes, and if she was late for social studies, Mr. Cole would be furious. Sometimes he sent kids straight to the office for walking in late, without even listening to excuses.

She looked around the media center frantically, hoping to find Brenda. She was the only one who could stop the paper from being passed out.

At last, Stephanie saw her standing beside a laser printer, pulling off pages as they spit out into a tray.

Stephanie flew across the room.

Brenda saw her coming and frowned at her. "What's your big rush?"

"I have to talk to you," Stephanie choked out.

"I'm busy now," Brenda said, straightening a stack of pages and handing them to another girl for collating.

"I know, and I really am sorry, but you can't sell this issue."

Brenda stopped what she was doing and turned to face Stephanie. "What are you talking about?"

"It has . . . it has some problems with it . . . in my column, actually." Stephanie was beginning to feel more nervous by the second. She wondered if she was going to get kicked off the staff right then and there.

"What's wrong with your column?" Brenda said.

Stephanie glanced at the bunch of student volunteers who had laid the stacks of pages on a long table and were assembling the paper. The last boy stapled the pages and added each copy to a growing pile.

Stephanie swallowed hard. "There are two things, actually," she began, her voice shaking. "You added that bit about the note."

Brenda smiled. "So?"

"Well, that was Darcy, and she's one of my closest friends. She was furious with me for putting stuff about her and Jerry in the paper the first time. So I promised her I wouldn't do it again."

Brenda looked amused. "Oh, boy, is she ever going to be ticked off when she sees this."

Stephanie let out a long sigh of relief. So Brenda understood. Maybe things would be okay after all. "She sure is going to be steamed," she said. "But it isn't even my fault because I didn't put the item in. You did, and without telling me."

"I can see your point," Brenda said reasonably. "What's the other problem?"

"The story about Tom and Polly. I have a feeling there was nothing going on between them."

"But I thought you checked out all your stories," Brenda said.

"I didn't think I had to check that one out. I mean, no one had seen Cheryl with Tom for weeks, and then there was Polly with him at the bus stop. It just seemed to make sense. Anyway, I didn't see any harm in it."

"I don't either," Brenda said. "Now I have to get back to work or these papers won't get out this afternoon."

She started to turn away but Stephanie tugged on her arm. "Wait, can't we add something to say the stories aren't true or they were printed by mistake?"

"You mean, like a retraction?" Brenda asked. She straightened up and glared down her wide nose at Stephanie. "No way. I don't see what the big deal is. It's only a gossip column. Besides, there isn't time. In an hour these copies will be on sale in the cafeteria."

An icy chill crushed through Stephanie. Darcy would never, ever speak to her again if she saw that column.

"What about if we just pull the page The Secret's Out is on? You can still sell the rest of the paper, and I'll do a double column for the next issue."

Brenda made a face and shook her head. "Tanner, you're overreacting. A little rumor in a newspaper isn't going to kill anyone. Darcy will get over it, and so will Cheryl."

"But—"

"The answer is no," Brenda said firmly. "We're coming out with this issue on time, with all its pages."

Stephanie looked up at the clock just as the late bell rang. Now she was in even more trouble, if that was possible. With a feeling of doom closing in around her, she trudged off to class.

Maybe she would quit the newspaper staff.
Maybe that was the only thing she could do, now
that she'd made such a mess of everything.

As soon as the dismissal bell rang at the end of
the day, Stephanie took off for Darcy's locker, hoping she could intercept her and Allie there. If she
could steer Darcy away from the cafeteria and
through the front door of the school, she might
keep her from reading the newspaper.

As Stephanie saw it, that was the only way of
saving her friendship with Darcy. But that also
meant she'd have to stop Allie, too. If Allie saw
the item in the column, she'd feel she had to tell
Darcy. And Stephanie couldn't blame her; she'd
probably do the same thing.

Stephanie tore down the hall, only slowing down
when she saw Mr. Thomas, the principal, walking
ahead of her. She slowed to a speed walk, and
when he stepped into a classroom, she picked up
her pace and ran the rest of the way. As she skidded around the corner, she saw her friends' heads
in the crowd. A tingle of relief rushed through her.

Made it! she thought happily. *Now if I can just
get them out the front door without a newspaper.*

But when she was only ten feet away from them,

a boy stepped aside, and she could see that Darcy was holding a copy of the *Scribe*.

Stephanie came to a screeching halt, her mouth suddenly dry, her hands shaking. "Oh, gosh," she breathed.

She thought about turning around and heading back the way she'd come. How could she ever face Darcy now? But she couldn't run away, either.

Maybe there was something she could say to make Darcy feel better. Or maybe Darcy hadn't even seen The Secret's Out yet and she could still get the paper away from her in time.

Quickly Stephanie raced up to the other two girls and immediately blurted out, "Hey, I heard the paper is really boring this time." She reached for the pages in Darcy's hands.

Darcy backed away from her, pulling the newspaper out of reach. "You promised!" she said. "You told me you wouldn't say anything about me and Jerry again. You promised."

"I—I didn't do anything wrong!" Stephanie objected. "That stuff about Jerry and the note, Brenda stuck it in there without even telling me! I swear. I swear on every Keanu Reeves movie we've ever seen!"

Darcy shook her head sadly. "Then how did

Brenda get the information to print in the first place? She wasn't in that classroom with us!"

"I know. It was something I wrote before, but she cut it. I guess she just stuck it into this issue as a filler. I was sort of short on material." Stephanie turned desperately to Allie. "Tell her . . . tell Darcy how hard it was to come up with stuff."

Allie looked torn between her two friends. "I helped Stephanie think up items for this week's column. It really was tough."

Darcy glared at Allie. "You told her it was all right to print this thing about me and Jerry?" She looked as if she'd strangle Allie, after she got done with Stephanie.

"No! Of course I didn't. That wasn't part of the column we wrote." Allie looked confused as she turned back to Stephanie. "Your editor really stuck that on the end without asking you?"

"Of course she did," Stephanie insisted. "I wouldn't do something like that after promising Darcy I wouldn't."

Allie sighed. "Well, I guess I wasn't very much help. I thought the part about Tom and Polly was going to be okay, too. But I saw Cheryl Craft in the girls' locker room fifth period, and she was crying."

Stephanie couldn't have felt worse at that moment. "I really didn't mean to hurt anyone," she repeated weakly. "I just thought—"

"You could have called Cheryl or Tom on the phone and asked them if they'd broken up," Darcy pointed out.

Stephanie bit down on her lip. She'd gotten so totally carried away by her own popularity and seeing her column in print that she'd stopped thinking about anybody else. Like the way the readers might feel when she printed personal things about them. Now she'd broken up two really special friendships, and hurt a lot of other people's feelings along the way.

She looked up at Darcy one last time, wishing her friend would just yell at her, once and for all, and get it out of her system.

Darcy glared at her, but when she spoke, her voice was soft. "I don't know what to think about you anymore," she said. "I don't think I can ever trust you again. You've just gone too far. Don't call me anymore. I don't want to be friends with someone I can't trust."

Stephanie watched in horror as Darcy closed her locker and walked away. "This is terrible," she muttered.

Stephanie looked at Allie, then at Darcy's retreating back. Darcy's shoulders were shaking. Stephanie was sure their friend was crying.

"I'd better go with her," Allie said.

"But *you* know I didn't do anything wrong this time," Stephanie choked out. "You were there with me when I put the column together!"

Allie stared unhappily at her Doc Martens. "I guess. But Darcy really needs a friend right now."

Stephanie watched Allie run off to catch up with Darcy. She collapsed against the lockers as the two girls disappeared into the crowd of kids leaving school for the day. "My whole life is ruined," she whispered.

CHAPTER
11

◆ ◢ ◈ ◆

Staring at the mound of steaming spaghetti on her plate, Stephanie pushed a meatball around it with her fork.

"Aren't you going to eat, sweetheart?" her father asked. "I made spaghetti because it's one of your favorites."

"I know you did, Dad," Stephanie said glumly. "Thanks."

"It's my favorite too," Michelle chimed in.

"Mine!" Nicky shouted.

"Mine!" Alex stabbed a meatball with his fork and waved it over his head. The meatball flew through the air and landed on the floor, right at Comet's feet. The dog wolfed it down and licked his chops.

Danny laughed. "Looks like it's one of Comet's favorites, too."

"Yeah." Stephanie sighed and pushed away her plate. "I know it's good, Dad. I'm sorry. I guess I'm just not hungry."

Danny looked at her. "Are you still having problems about that Fun City story?."

"Yes, but it's not just that one," Stephanie said. "Things are even more complicated now."

"Fun City!" Michelle said excitedly. "We're going this Saturday, right, Dad?"

"Right, Michelle," Danny said. He turned back to Stephanie. "Do you want to talk about it, honey?"

Stephanie shook her head. "I think I'll just go lie down for a little while. I don't feel very well."

Up in her room, Stephanie lay on her bed and stared at the ceiling, hot tears clinging to her eyelashes. No matter how hard she tried to work things out, they only got worse.

Half an hour later, there was a knock on her door.

"May I come in?" a voice asked. It was Aunt Becky.

She walked slowly across the room that Stephanie shared with Michelle and sat on the edge of the bed.

"Feel like talking yet?" Becky asked.

"Not really," Stephanie said. "Talking won't make anything better."

"It could. I mean, I might have some ideas about how to make things right."

Stephanie took a deep breath. She really did want to talk to someone, but she was ashamed of what she'd done. And she hated to admit all the mistakes she'd made, especially to Becky, who always seemed to have her act together.

"Thanks, Becky. Maybe later," Stephanie whispered.

Becky smoothed the hair away from Stephanie's face and smiled gently at her. "Well, I'll be here if you need me."

Stephanie rolled over to face the wall. She'd really blown it big this time. Mr. Assante was disappointed in her and the whole class was going to be mad about the Fun City trip.

And Darcy? What could she do now to make Darcy forgive her?

Then there was Cheryl.

How many ways can one person mess up? she thought miserably.

Stephanie squeezed her eyes shut, wishing the world would go away. She knew she should be starting her homework, but there was no way she'd ever be able to concentrate.

"Knock knock!" a voice called from the other side of the bedroom door.

"Go away, D.J.," Stephanie called out weakly. "I don't want to watch TV with you or do anything right now."

D.J. ignored her and walked into the room anyway.

Stephanie turned around, prepared to yell at her to get out. Then she saw the tray in her sister's hands—loaded with a big plastic bowl of popcorn and two tall glasses of soda.

Suddenly Stephanie felt enormously hungry and thirsty.

"I know we're not supposed to have food in our rooms," D.J. said, "but I figured you must be getting pretty hungry. And it's hard to think on an empty stomach."

"I've given up thinking," Stephanie moaned, sitting up on her bed. "There's just no way out of this."

"Out of what?" D.J. asked.

Stephanie took a handful of the warm, buttery popcorn. She popped a piece into her mouth, and it tasted wonderful. She took a sip of cola.

"I've made a mess of things, and now no one's talking to me. At least no one I really care about."

"Darcy and Allie?" D.J. asked.

"Right." She tossed a fistful of popcorn into her mouth all at once. "The trouble started with my writing the gossip column for the *Scribe*."

"I kind of guessed that," D.J. said. "But I thought it was going great. A couple of my friends at school were talking about it. . . ."

"Really? They heard about my column in the high school?" Stephanie couldn't help feeling pleased. Then she reminded herself how much trouble she had already gotten herself into.

"Yeah," D.J. said, "some of them have brothers and sisters who brought the paper home. They saw your name in it and asked if you were related to me."

"You probably said *no*," Stephanie said.

D.J. laughed. "Of course I told them you were my sister! I'm proud of you!"

"You are? Really?" Stephanie smiled. "But see, I used some pretty shaky stories, and others weren't even true. The one about Darcy and Jerry was supposed to be private." She told D.J. all about her other stories. "I had no business telling the whole school any of those things."

"I know," D.J. agreed. "It wasn't the smartest move you've ever made. So what are you going to do now?"

"Now?" Stephanie shook her head. "How about you lend me money for a trip to Mexico? I'll start a new life there."

D.J. laughed. "It's not that bad. You just have to make things right for everyone."

"How?"

"Well, you can quit the paper and hope that's enough to show your friends that you're honestly sorry. Then promise them you won't write anything embarrassing about them ever again."

"I don't want to be a quitter. That's what the last three writers for The Secret's Out did. I keep thinking there must be some way to do it right."

D.J. nodded. "That's a good way of looking at it. Well, your only other option is to do something nice to make up for the bad stuff."

"I've tried saying I'm sorry, but nobody listens," Stephanie said. "The best thing would be to get Jerry and Darcy back together and patch things up for Cheryl and Tom." She thought a moment. "You know, maybe that's what I should try to do instead of just apologizing. If I could figure out a way to do it, that is. I mean, Darcy and Jerry are avoiding each other the way Comet runs from a bath."

"They're probably too embarrassed to talk," D.J. said.

"Yeah, what I have to do is get them together so they *have* to talk."

Just then, Michelle burst into the room and screeched to a halt when she saw her sisters sitting on the bed with the bowl of popcorn between them. "I'm telling!" she threatened, backing toward the door.

D.J. jumped up and stopped her before she could reach the hall. She stood in the doorway, eyeing her little sister. "We're being very careful. Besides, Stephanie needed nourishment. She didn't have any dinner."

"So what!" Michelle said. "A rule is a rule."

"Okay," D.J. said, winking at Stephanie, "go ahead and tell. I guess that means I should tell Dad about the bag of gummy worms you keep hidden in your socks drawer." She nodded at the bureau.

Michelle narrowed her eyes at her. "You wouldn't."

"Try me," D.J. said.

"Oh, all right." Michelle sighed dramatically and left the room. When she'd gone, Stephanie looked at D.J. "You really think I can find ways to get everyone back together again?"

"Sure you can," D.J. said. "And if they really like each other, they'll talk things out. Then you just have to be more careful about what you write from now on."

"I sure will," Stephanie said as she watched D.J. sneak out the door with the remains of their snack on the tray.

She leaned back against her pillow. *Getting people together to talk might work,* she thought. Now she just had to figure out a way to do it.

As soon as Stephanie got to school Friday morning, she went in search of Jerry Wilkes. She looked around his locker but didn't see him there. She found a couple of boys who knew him and asked them where he was, but they hadn't seen him yet that day.

At last, she peeked into the media center. He was seated at a table in the far corner, a book in his hands, his thick-rimmed glasses sliding down the bridge of his nose.

Taking a deep breath and wishing herself good luck, Stephanie moved quietly through the door to where Jerry sat.

She stood over him. "Jerry? Can I talk to you for a minute?"

Jerry looked up at her with a blank expression. "I've got reading to finish before English class." He concentrated on the book again.

Stephanie pulled up a chair beside his. "This is important. It's about Darcy."

"Darcy thinks I'm a creep. She doesn't want anything to do with me," he mumbled.

"She doesn't think you're a creep!" Stephanie assured him. "She thinks you're a cool guy. She told me herself how she likes your sense of humor and how smart you are."

He blinked at her, then frowned. "She told you that?"

"Honest." Stephanie swallowed and quickly went on. "The thing is, even though she likes you, she was a little shy about telling the whole world right away—you know, about how she felt about you. I blabbed it all in my column, and that shook her up."

Jerry nodded thoughtfully. "Well, maybe it's for the best anyway. Darcy's a really popular girl. She

106

doesn't want to hang out with a nerd like me. Or was it a geek you called me?"

Stephanie winced. "I'm really sorry, Jerry. I just got carried away when I was writing. I didn't mean to hurt your feelings."

Jerry sighed and closed his book. "Well, okay."

"And you're not a geek at all; it's just that I didn't know you very well. I can see why Darcy likes you. You're nice and intelligent. I'd love to hear you play your drums sometime."

"You would?" he asked, a look of surprise on his face.

"Sure. Darcy too!"

Jerry stood up to go to his classroom.

"Listen, I have an idea," Stephanie said, falling into step beside him. "Why don't we give you and Darcy a chance to talk things over? You can come over to my house, and I'll find a way to get her there, too."

Jerry smiled and nudged his heavy glasses up his nose. "You think she'd really come?"

"Yup," Stephanie said, sounding a lot more sure of herself than she felt. "Listen, I gotta go, but I'll catch you later at my house. Come over right after school."

She spotted Allie at the other end of the hall and

followed her. Allie turned into a classroom, which Stephanie recognized as Darcy's homeroom. Darcy was seated in the last row, finishing some homework, while Allie stood over her, talking to her.

Stephanie glanced up at the homeroom teacher, who seemed busy with her own paperwork. She rushed over to Darcy's desk.

"Hi!" she said, stooping down beside her so that Darcy couldn't slip out of her seat to avoid her. "I know you're still mad at me, and I don't blame you a bit. Even though this time it wasn't my fault."

"I heard from some other kids on the newspaper staff what Brenda did," Darcy said stiffly. "But you know, Steph, if you hadn't written the story in the first place, none of this would have happened."

Stephanie winced. She hated when Darcy used that hurt tone of voice. "I know, and I want to make things up to you," she said. "Come over my house after school, okay? We'll bake brownies together and pig out, just like old times."

"I don't know," Darcy murmured, avoiding her eyes.

"Please? I really want to make up to you for what I did." Stephanie held her breath.

"Okay," Darcy agreed at last, with a hesitant smile. "But I have to stop off at my house first, to tell my mom where I'll be."

All right! Stephanie thought triumphantly. But she didn't dare say it out loud. Forcing herself to remain calm, she stood up. "Great. I'll see you at my house around three thirty."

As Stephanie raced for her own homeroom, she felt much better. Of course, she hadn't solved the problem between Darcy and Jerry yet. And she still had to do something about Cheryl and Tom, and the Fun City trip. Fixing things wasn't going to be easy, but there was no way she'd give up!

CHAPTER

12

◆ ◢ ◣ ◆

Stephanie marched through the front door and straight into the kitchen. Michelle was sitting at the table munching on a cookie, with a glass of milk close at hand.

"Do we still have any of those chocolate-chip cookies?" Stephanie asked breathlessly as she opened and closed cupboards.

"You mean the ones Darcy likes?" Michelle asked.

"Yeah. The kind with the minichips in them."

"I think Becky put them in the cookie jar."

"Great!" Stephanie dove for the teddy-bear-shaped jar on the counter, her heart racing. She wanted to get everything ready before Jerry, Allie, and Darcy arrived. If she handled the meeting between Darcy and Jerry just right, maybe everybody could be friends again.

There were just enough chocolate-chip cookies to make a nice size plate for the table. She even poured milk into a pretty pitcher and set it out with glasses and napkins.

Barely taking a breath, she tore up the stairs to her room, dumped her book bag on the bed, and ran a brush through her hair.

The doorbell rang.

"I'll get it!" Michelle shouted.

Stephanie nervously closed her eyes and took three deep breaths. "Please let this work. Please, please let this work!" she murmured.

"It's a boy!" Michelle yelled up the stairs.

Jerry! Stephanie thought. She'd been hoping he'd arrive first. That way Darcy couldn't run into him on her way to the house. If she'd seen him along the way, she might change her mind about coming.

Stephanie bolted down the stairs two at a time.

"Is she here yet?" Jerry asked, nervously shifting from foot to foot. He was wearing a Soul Asylum T-shirt and a jean jacket.

"No, you're first."

"Darcy probably won't come anyway," Jerry said sadly. "She hates me."

"She doesn't hate you, believe me," Stephanie said. "She's just upset, and that's all my fault, not yours."

"If you say so," Jerry said. He looked around the living room. "Hey, this is a nice house."

"Want to see my room?" Michelle offered cheerfully. "I share with Stephanie."

Stephanie was horrified, thinking of the pajamas she'd flung on her bed that morning while dressing. "Of course he doesn't want to see our room!" She quickly steered Jerry toward the kitchen. "You wait in there. Darcy should be here any minute. There's a snack all ready on the table."

"Thanks," Jerry said. "I am a little hungry."

No sooner had he disappeared through the kitchen door than the bell rang a second time.

Michelle leaped for the door. "I'll ge—"

"No, you won't!" Stephanie shouted. "Don't you have something to do?" she asked Michelle pointedly.

Michelle sighed. "I guess I'll go upstairs and play dolls . . . all by myself."

The bell rang a second time. As soon as Michelle was out of sight, Stephanie swung the door wide.

112

"Hi, Darcy!" Stephanie said. "Come on in."

Following Stephanie inside, Darcy took off her jacket and laid it across the arm of the couch. Stephanie counted herself lucky that Jerry had kept his on. If Darcy had seen it before Stephanie had a chance to explain, she'd have been out the door like a shot.

Darcy smiled a little. "So. Are we going to make brownies?"

Stephanie ran her tongue over her lips. "Uh, well," she said, her throat closing up on her words. She coughed to clear it. "First, I want to talk about you and—"

"Is she here yet?" Jerry called from the kitchen.

Darcy stared at the kitchen door, looking suddenly nervous. "Who's that?"

The door swung open, and Jerry strode into the living room. He was chewing on a mouthful of cookies and held a glass of milk in one hand. "Hey, good, you got here, Darcy! I poured some milk for you."

Darcy took a shaky step backward. "I—I can't believe you did this!" she choked out, staring wide-eyed at Stephanie.

"I just wanted you two to be able to talk," Stephanie explained desperately. "It was all my fault you stopped studying with Jerry, and I want to make things right again."

Darcy stared at her in horror. "You lied to me! You tricked me into coming here to embarrass me."

"No!" Stephanie protested. "I wouldn't do—"

"I'll never, ever talk to you as long as I live!" Darcy sobbed, backing quickly toward the door. "Never!"

Stephanie didn't know what to do, she felt so bad. It wasn't until a second later that she realized Jerry had rushed across the room, spilling half of his milk on the way. He grabbed Darcy by the arm before she could step outside and swung her around.

Darcy looked startled.

"Wait," he said, setting his glass on a table beside the door. "This whole thing has gotten totally blown out of proportion. If you don't want your friends to see us together, I understand. You're super-popular, and everyone thinks I'm just a nerd."

Darcy stared at Jerry, her expression softening. "I don't think you're a nerd. You're a nice guy, and you're smart. I liked studying with you."

He shrugged. "You don't have to say that just to make me feel better. I don't have any bad feel-

114

ings about you, Darcy. I just wish we could have stayed friends and kept on studying together."

Darcy blinked guiltily at him. She looked at Stephanie, then back at Jerry.

"I—I really would like to get together with you again," Darcy said shyly.

"You would?" Jerry looked amazed. He grinned at her.

"Yeah. How about Monday, after school, at the library?"

"Sure, that'd be great!" He turned to Stephanie and nodded at her. "Thanks for asking me over. I should go now; I have a drum lesson."

After he'd left, Stephanie picked up his glass and took it out to the kitchen. When she came back into the living room, Darcy was still there.

"I want to talk to you, Stephanie," Darcy said solemnly.

Stephanie sighed and started wiping up the spilled milk from the carpet with paper towels. "You're still mad at me, aren't you?"

Darcy sat down beside her on the floor. "No. I need to apologize to you."

"*You* need to apologize to *me?*" Stephanie gasped.

"See, there's been more than one reason I've

been avoiding you for the past few weeks," Darcy admitted. "I was mad at you because you gossiped about me, but there was another reason."

"What's that?" Stephanie asked, curious.

"I stayed away from you because I couldn't admit the truth to you, or myself. I wasn't brave enough to go out with a guy like Jerry, who isn't exactly the most popular kid in school. I guess I didn't want anyone to know that I had a crush on a guy who isn't supposed to be cool—at least not in the way a lot of kids think is cool."

"So you were afraid of being seen with him?"

"Right." Darcy slowly shook her head. "I just didn't want you to figure out the truth, and I feel terrible for treating Jerry so badly. He's really nice."

"Well, it wasn't fair for me to call Jerry a nerd and a geek, either. Words like nerd and geek can be mean. You're right, Darce, he is nice. I just got carried away, trying to be super-popular by coming up with exciting stories. I never meant to hurt anyone." Stephanie touched Darcy on the arm. "You forgive me?"

Darcy smiled and nodded. "Yeah. I guess we both blew it, trying to be popular. It's kind of more important to be a good friend."

*　　*　　*

After Darcy left, Stephanie went up to her room, already thinking of the next part of her plan. Tom and Cheryl. She had to do something to make things right with them. Well, why not use the gossip column?

Sitting down at her desk, she took out a clean sheet of paper. She thought a moment, then started writing. After a few minutes, she sat back in her chair and let out a long breath.

"I hope this does the trick," she whispered.

No. She changed her mind. *Writing a new item for The Secret's Out isn't enough,* she decided.

She took her copy of the column with her into D.J.'s room and closed the door. Then she looked up Cheryl's phone number and dialed it.

Mrs. Craft picked up the phone, and Stephanie asked for Cheryl.

"She's out in the backyard with her brother," Cheryl's mom said. "Hold on and I'll call her for you."

"Thanks." Stephanie chewed her fingernail nervously. She was afraid Cheryl might hang up on her as soon as she realized who had called.

"Hello?" a voice said from the other end.

"Hi, Cheryl, this is Stephanie Tanner."

"Oh," Cheryl said, in a quiet voice. "What do you want?"

Stephanie took a deep breath. "I want to apologize for printing that story in the paper about Tom and Polly. It wasn't true, at least not the part about them dating."

"Well, it really doesn't matter," Cheryl said. "We sort of had a big fight."

Stephanie winced. "Listen, I *am* sorry, and I have something to read to you that might make things better."

"I don't think anything can—"

"Just listen," Stephanie pleaded. "It's a new item for my next column of the Secret's Out."

She started reading before Cheryl could object.

"The secret's out about the *real* love of T.A.'s life. He may be willing to share an umbrella with a friend in a storm, but he'd rather hold hands with C.C. any day. This reporter can't wait to see them together again."

For a long moment, Stephanie heard only silence on the other end of the phone line, then Cheryl said softly, "That's sweet, Steph. I like it a lot. You mean, Tom never really had a date with Polly?"

"Not with Polly or anyone else, as far as this reporter knows!" Stephanie said.

"That's great." But Cheryl's voice seemed to be growing fainter. "I said some pretty mean things to him. I wonder if he'll forgive me. Maybe I'll call him and see if we can get back together.''

After she hung up, Stephanie glanced down at the item she'd just written, feeling pleased with herself. But her smile only lasted for a few minutes.

She remembered the one thing she hadn't been able to set right—the seventh-grade party. How could she possibly get her class into Fun City?

CHAPTER
13

◆ ◀ ◗ ◆

On Saturday morning, Stephanie got together with Darcy and Allie, and they helped her put together a new column. It included the item about Cheryl and Tom, a piece about the field trip the eighth grade was planning to the planetarium, a few sentences about Mr. Dempsey, a math teacher who was leaving the school to teach for a year in Japan, and some gossip about a new student.

It was what Darcy called "good gossip." Angela Franco had broken the girls' hundred-meter track record at her old school, and it was rumored that Coach Yancy thought she'd break John Muir Middle School's record too and go on to run in state finals. Stephanie had gone straight to Coach and asked if the rumor was true, and he'd verified the facts. He added he was thrilled that Angela would be running for their school.

"It's not exactly as exciting as your other columns," Brenda complained when Stephanie read the column to her over the phone. "But I guess this stuff's interesting enough to run."

"Good," Stephanie said, "because it's all news that will make everyone happy."

"Sure you couldn't dig up some dirt on anyone?" Brenda asked.

Stephanie smiled to herself. "I hear you and Lenny Twilling are going to the eighth-grade dance together. Maybe we could print that!"

"*Me*, go with a seventh grader?" Brenda gasped. "I'd kill you if you put that in your column! It's a good thing I'm the editor."

Stephanie laughed. "It's not so much fun when you're the one being gossiped about, is it?"

There was a moment of silence from the other end of the line. "Just don't get too sure of yourself, Stephanie Tanner," Brenda grumbled. "I can still kick you off this newspaper staff if I want to."

* * *

Later that morning, Danny, Joey, Michelle, D.J., and Stephanie piled into the car and headed for Fun City. Michelle was so excited she could hardly sit still, but Stephanie was kind of quiet. Danny finally noticed and asked her why.

Stephanie sighed. "It's just every time I go on one of the rides, I'll be thinking how much fun my friends would have if they could go on them at our class party."

"Cheer up," Michelle said. "All we get in third grade for a party is cold pizza and warm soda in our classroom."

Stephanie smiled at her. "Thanks for trying to cheer me up, but I feel as if I've let everyone down."

In the driver's seat, Danny glanced at her in the rearview mirror. "I'm sorry there's nothing I can do to help you, sweetheart."

"Are you sure you can't think of *something*, Dad?" she asked.

"I might be able to swing a couple of passes, but over eighty of them?" He shook his head.

"I'd contribute to the ticket fund, but I could only add two or three more," Joey said.

"That's okay." Stephanie shrugged. "I guess it's a lost cause."

The park was even more exciting than Stephanie

had imagined. After walking past a long arcade jammed with noisy, flashing video games, they turned into a midway filled with exciting rides. The crowd was so thick, Stephanie had to squeeze between people to keep up with Danny and the others.

The air smelled of popcorn, cotton candy, and hot dogs. Joey was in an especially great mood, rattling off jokes to Michelle as they strolled along, talking about which rides they wanted to try first.

"I've got to get up on that cable car that crosses the whole park," Danny said, craning his neck to look at the brightly painted cars passing over their heads.

"The bumper cars! The bumper cars!" Michelle cried, jumping up and down and pointing.

Joey eyed a stand that was selling foot-long hot dogs. "What does a five-hundred-pound canary eat?" he asked Michelle.

"Anything he wants!" They all shouted out the punch line, laughing.

They started with the bumper cars to keep Michelle happy. After that, D.J. and Stephanie rode the gigantic merry-go-round with her.

"Let's try something in the arcade," Michelle said.

"What game do you want to play?" Joey asked her.

"I'm not sure," Michelle said. "Go Fish would be fun." Her eyes roamed the midway and lit up when they hit the candy apple booth. "Boy, those look yummy."

Joey winked at the others. "Michelle, why don't you and I go fish, then stop for a snack? We'll meet the others in an hour back at the bumper cars."

"Cool!" Michelle shouted.

Stephanie waved at Michelle as she and Joey took off toward the ticket line.

"What about you girls?" Danny asked. "I'm for a coffee break, myself. I'm pretty worn out."

D.J. looked around. "I want to have my fortune read." She pointed to a booth halfway down the midway. The sign said: *Madam Zoltar Knows All.*

Danny laughed. "That's a hoax. No one can tell the future."

Except me, Stephanie thought. *The kids at school are going to think I'm a creep for making up the party story.*

"I know it's just pretend," D.J. admitted. "But it's still fun! You coming, Steph?"

"No," she said. "I think I'll just walk around and see what the rest of the place looks like. Meet you at the bumper cars."

A few minutes later, Stephanie stopped and stared at a sign beside one of the rides: *Win a Full-Day Pass to Fun City.*

Stephanie's heart raced. Could this be true? She looked at the sign and read on.

You fly, we buy. If you have what it takes to ride the Tyrannosaur roller coaster three times, you get a free day at Fun City.

"Wow!" she breathed. "Just three times?"

She didn't much care for roller coasters. They made her stomach feel a little sick, even when she hadn't eaten anything before climbing aboard. But if all it took to win a pass was three rides . . . Hey, no sweat!

Stephanie did some quick arithmetic. Eighty-seven kids in her class. To get eighty-seven free passes, all she had to do was ride . . . three times eighty-seven . . . two hundred sixty-one times!

Her stomach felt a little queasy already, just thinking about the prospect of riding the roller coaster that many times. But maybe it wouldn't be so bad. And at least she'd be handling the problem on her own.

She walked over to the line to wait her turn. It wasn't very long, for some reason. She wondered if that was because a lot of kids were afraid to ride it.

"Excuse me," she said when she reached the gate where an attendant was helping people get into cars and locking the safety bar across their laps. "I want to go for the free pass. Do I have to sign up or anything?"

"No," the girl said, "but I need to give you a special card. We punch it every time you ride. When it's been punched three times, you get your free pass." She handed Stephanie a bright orange card.

Stephanie pulled a pen from her backpack and wrote her name at the top of the card. Just as she stuck the card and pen in her pack, the ride started moving.

"Here goes," she murmured, gripping the safety bar.

The first half of the ride wasn't bad at all. The cars went up and down a lot, and people giggled nervously. A couple of girls screamed, but Stephanie didn't think it was very scary. Then there was a series of sharp turns that made her feel as if she was being jolted out of her seat, but the bar held her in place.

She saw her father walking across the midway, and he raised his paper cup of coffee to her.

"No sweat!" she shouted at him from the gradual hill they'd started climbing.

Danny laughed at her and pointed up ahead. When she looked, all she could see was a long incline continuing up and up and up. It looked as if it was reaching up into the clouds.

Stephanie swallowed.

"Here comes the big one!" a boy behind her shouted.

A few seconds later, the car reached the top of the hill and Stephanie looked down. The people below looked like insects, and the roller-coaster track seemed to drop off into thin air.

She screamed . . . and she kept on screaming all the way to the bottom as her stomach crammed itself into her throat and her knuckles turned white from gripping the safety bar. She was sure the car was going to fling itself off into space and she would never be seen again. It whipped around another corner, then up and down two more hills.

Finally the cars stopped. Stephanie gasped for breath and looked around. People were getting off the ride. It was over. She'd survived after all.

"How was it?" her father asked when she staggered through the exit gate.

Stephanie forced a smile. "Great. I think I'll go on again."

"Kids!" Danny said with a laugh. "Okay, have fun, sweetheart. Just don't make yourself sick. I'll see you later."

Gripping her orange card, Stephanie turned back through the admission gate to wait for her second ride.

By the third ride she was feeling a little queasy, and the world seemed to be spinning lazily around her. But she exchanged her punched ticket for a free day pass.

"One down," she murmured, feeling more determined than ever. "Eighty-six to go." Maybe she could come here every day after school for a month and just keep on riding the Tyrannosaur. That way she'd have free passes for the whole class by the time of the party.

"You really like this ride, don't you?" the attendant said as she lowered the bar over Stephanie's lap for her fourth ride.

"Yeah," she said with a weak smile. "It's great. May I please have another orange card?"

The girl grinned. "Sure. Have a ball!"

When Stephanie stepped off at the end of ride, she was sure the cars had been moving faster than the other three times. She was feeling even more woozy, and her stomach had begun to hurt.

"Hey, we were watching you!" Michelle called to her from the gate when she headed back to get in line for ride number five. "That ride looks really exciting."

"You can say that again," Stephanie said.

Joey put out a hand and stopped her. "Hey, Steph, you don't look so good. Sure you want to go for another spin?"

"I have to," she said.

"Huh?" Joey looked confused.

"See the sign?" she said, pointing. "Every time I finish three rides, I get a free pass. Since there's no other way to earn them for my class, I'm doing it this way."

"Cool!" Michelle cried. "Can I help?"

They decided that Michelle could work on a card

too if Joey sat with her to make sure she was all right. At the end of an hour, they had a total of four passes.

Stephanie, Michelle, and Joey turned to get back in line again. All three of them were walking funny now. Stephanie was in a daze. Then, from a distance, she heard someone shouting their names.

She turned to see Danny and D.J. on the other side of the fence.

"What are you guys doing?" D.J. asked. "You've been on the same ride all afternoon! And you look like you're going to barf."

"It's not really that bad," Joey explained solemnly, blinking to clear his vision. "We're just helping Steph out."

"Yeah," Stephanie said, "it's working out great, Dad." She held up their three passes as the park spun around her. "Only eighty-four passes to go, and the whole class can come."

Danny reached out and grabbed her before she could fall over. He looked at her with concern. "You guys can't keep this up. Come with me. I have an idea."

* * *

The following Monday in school, Stephanie was feeling a lot better. She hunted down Mr. Assante in his classroom and handed him an envelope.

"What's this?" he asked.

"Half-price coupons for Fun City," she explained proudly. "They would have been free tickets, but my dad didn't think I'd live long enough to earn them."

Mr. Assante laughed at her. "Stephanie, what are you talking about?"

"My family and I went to Fun City over the weekend." She went on to explain her plan to win free passes for her whole class. "The manager of the amusement park was so impressed with the way my family and I were trying to earn passes for my class, he gave us ninety half-price coupons. It's good advertising for him, and now we can afford to go to Fun City for the party."

"Well, I guess we can!" he said, shaking his head in amazement.

By lunchtime word had gotten out that the seventh-grade class party at Fun City was on. Everyone was talking about it, and Stephanie couldn't have been happier.

She found an empty table in a corner of the cafeteria and sat down to write her next col-

umn for the *Scribe*. It was going to blow everyone away!

*The seventh grade will party all day on December
15 at Fun City, thanks to Mr. Costello of Fun City,
Incorporated.*

*D.P. and J.W. are really, truly an item now—and
they say they don't care who knows it!*

S.T., D.P., and A.T. are best friends forever!

YOU COULD WIN
A VISIT TO THE WARNER BROS. STUDIO!

One First Prize: Trip for up to three people to the Warner Bros. Studios in Burbank, CA, home of the "Full House" Set

Ten Second Prizes: "Stephanie" posters autographed by actress Jodi Sweetin

Twenty-Five Third Prizes: One "Full House" Stephanie Boxed Set

Name_____ Birthdate_____

Address_____

City_____ State____ Zip_____

Daytime Phone_____

POCKET BOOKS/"Full House" SWEEPSTAKES

OUTSTANDING AND UNIQUE!
INCREDIBLE! ELITE!
THEY'LL SWEEP YOU OFF YOUR FEET!
GO PATTI! GO CASSIE!
GO LAUREN! GO TARA!

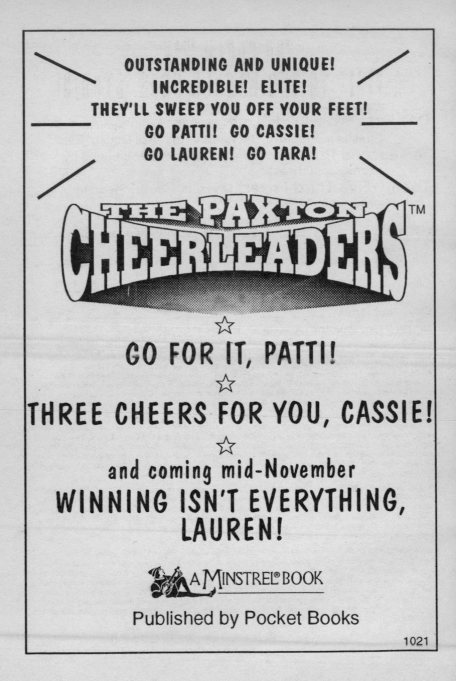

THE PAXTON™ CHEERLEADERS

☆

GO FOR IT, PATTI!

☆

THREE CHEERS FOR YOU, CASSIE!

☆

and coming mid-November
WINNING ISN'T EVERYTHING, LAUREN!

A MINSTREL® BOOK

Published by Pocket Books